My Tango with Barbara Strozzi

My Tango with Barbara Strozzi

RUSSELL HOBAN

BLOOMSBURY
LONDON · BERLIN · NEW YORK

First published 2007
This paperback edition published 2008

Copyright © 2007 by Russell Hoban

The moral right of the author has been asserted

Bloomsbury Publishing Plc,
36 Soho Square,
London W1D 3QY

A CIP catalogue record for this book is available from the British Library

ISBN 978 0 7475 9271 6

10 9 8 7 6 5 4 3 2 1

Typeset by Hewer Text UK Ltd, Edinburgh
Printed in Great Britain by Clays Ltd, St Ives plc

To Dr Michael D. Feher

'So there was the problem set for the sawyers – in a curved tree (butt or top it didn't matter) to find that one aspect of it which was not curved – that one direction in which it could be sawn into two practically equal and similar halves from end to end.'

The Wheelwright's Shop – George Sturt

PHIL OCKERMAN

When she told me that her name was Bertha Strunk I said, 'Is Bertha's trunk anything like Pandora's box?'

'That isn't something you can find out in five minutes,' she said. This was at the Saturday evening tango class for beginners in the crypt of St James's Church, Clerkenwell.

Why the tango? Are you sitting comfortably? It began with Mimi, my ex-wife, coming round with some things that I'd left at the house. 'Your latest effort got terrible reviews,' she said by way of greeting.

'The *Irish Times* and the *Jewish Chronicle* liked it,' I countered.

'I think you may be running out of ideas,' she said.

I backed away from her and made a cross with my fingers. 'Don't say that!'

'It happens,' she continued. '*Hope of a Tree* does not develop organically from its original impulse; it's a put-together thing trying to pass itself off as a novel. I have to go now. See you.'

'Please,' I said, 'be a stranger.'

When she left I had an awful dropped feeling in the pit of my stomach because I knew she was right. Altogether it was a delicate time for me; even before her visit I'd been uneasy about Pluto coming over my Sagittarian ascendant. 'This a major mega astrological event,' says Catriona, my astrologer. 'Your quest for a new theme could take a long time, with retrogradation and the slow moving of the outer planet. Euphemisms such as transformations, deaths and resurrections of the spirit and cleansing with reference to depth psychology are often used in connection with this; also crisis, power struggles etc. Definitely a time for the shedding of habits, feelings, emotions or whatever which have lost their vitality or relevance.' Thanks very much, Catriona. Most of my habits, feelings, emotions or whatever, probably all of them, have lost their vitality or relevance. 'Your Pluto is in house (8th) area which is its own, death, loss of individual etc.,' she goes on but I didn't.

I couldn't face the word machine and it was too early in the day to get drunk, so I went to the Royal Academy to look at the *Face the Music* exhibition: portraits of composers from all places and periods. Looking at various faces of those long dead I wondered how they'd feel about what's happened to some of their music. Here's Mozart, apparently without a care in the world. His *Piano Concerto 21* was taken over by the film

Elvira Madigan, the story of two doomed (by their own idiocy) young lovers, and will forever be associated with them by people ignorant even of the composer's name. The slow movement must by now be his most widely recognised composition. I'd recently acquired the DVD of the film and I sat patiently through it. Unmoved. Films go out of date like bacon on the supermarket shelf. I doubt very much that *Elvira Madigan* would win prizes if released this year even though Pia Degermark has (as film critic Roger Ebert has noted) beautiful calves.

Tchaikovsky now, magisterially bearded but looking doubtful – whatever his sins he didn't deserve what Ken Russell did to him with *The Music Lovers*. Did Russell hate the composer or what? Not that the film has much to do with Tchaikovsky, von Meck and the other famous names under which the actors perform as directed. The film is some kind of a lunatic thing with a life of its own that has little to do with any reality, not even Ken Russell's, whatever that may be. Pyotr Ilyich has suffered other indignities as well: some years ago his *Romeo and Juliet Overture* was mawkished into 'Our Love' and 'The Story of a Starry Night' and sung by various and sundry.

Vivaldi! He looks frail but he very aggressively put me on hold and kept me there while I trudged through as much of *Le Quatro Stagioni* as I could remember. Vivaldi, at a switchboard near you for how many more seasons?

So many names, so many faces, so much music! But wait, who's this? What does the card say? Barbara Strozzi, the seventeenth-century Venetian singer and composer who was known as *La Virtuosissima Cantatrice*. What a woman!

Not a beauty but she had a slightly sluttish look that was irresistible. Her eyes, so languorous, so not caring, so haunting after three centuries and more! She leans back in her chair, her blouse well off her shoulders, her bodice lowered to expose her breasts, her left hand grasping the neck of a viola da gamba. Barbara Strozzi! Dead for so many years but she reached out of the frame and clasped me to her opulent bosom and opened her mouth to my tongue. OK, it was all in my mind but so is everything else. Perhaps I fainted, I don't know. I didn't fall down but it was a Road-to-Damascus kind of thing. A girl of twelve or thirteen and her mother approached as I stood there. 'That man has an erection,' said the girl.

'Nonsense,' said the mother as they moved on. 'It's probably his iPod.'

I didn't want to see any more pictures so I left. When I got home I dug around in my CD stacks until I found my Barbara Strozzi discs. The tracks were mostly *lamentate*, lamentations. I played some of them but they didn't give me the Strozzi I'd seen in the portrait; they all had a downward spiral of sadness. OK, life *is* sad but the look in Barbara Strozzi's eyes had a whole lot more than sadness in it. I wanted other music for her. What kind of music?

When I think of Venice I think of Francesco Guardi. There is a page of his *macchiete* in *The Glory of Venice* catalogue from the Royal Academy. These quick sketches done in brown ink, almost calligraphy, show gaggles of men and women like brown leaves hurried on by the winds of time. Guardi's gondoliers, workmen and pedestrians in the oil paintings such as *The Giudecca with the Zitelle* are also full of movement, but of a stagey sort, as if they might be in an opera. It is particularly evident in pictures where chiaroscuro is exaggerated that Guardi is a precursor of Daumier: he paints gestures and peoples them, all of his figures moving through time. The buildings too, though solid and full of detail, are in motion through time. Sometimes this motion is slowed down, as in the wonderful *Capriccio with an Arch in Ruin*. Here Guardi's imagination is measured and reflective: even the dogs pause for thought and the boatmen are in no hurry. Although Barbara Strozzi was painted by Bernardo Strozzi (whose illegitimate daughter she probably was) there was something of a Guardi *capriccio* in the look she turned upon me through the transparent centuries. There was music in that look — not her own *lamentate* but something more coarse and sexual and a rhythm of controlled passion. I don't know the dances of Guardi's time and Strozzi's, but for me the music and the dance became tango.

I looked at her portrait in the catalogue again and words came to me, from where I couldn't remember: 'I faced up to life and . . . what?' My hand went to the

CD stacks and came up with Tita Merello, *Arrabalera*. The little brochure quoted her as saying, 'I faced up to life and it left its mark on me.' It sounds better in Spanish: '*Le di la cara a la vida y me la dejo marcada.*' I put the disc in the player and went to track 12, 'El Choclo'. Her voice! It wound itself around me like the *tanguera* that she was, like her body touching mine and leaning away, her leg gripping my waist and releasing in the skirmishing of the dance. Barbara Merello, Tita Strozzi!

So there it was: it was time for me to learn the tango if I wanted to follow the Barbara Strozzi thing wherever it might take me. A little googling brought me to To-taltango on the Internet and I sent away for *Dancing Tango*, a beginner's course by Christine Denniston on CD-ROM, with animations and video clips.

From the text of the CD I learned that at the end of the nineteenth century in Buenos Aires, a city with a huge influx of men from Spain, the best chance for a man to get his arms around a woman other than a prostitute was to learn the tango. The men attended *practicas* in which the learners danced with experienced men and with each other, alternately taking the part of the follower and that of the leader. They had to be able to dance as women before they could become good enough leaders to make a woman want to dance with them. When they were ready for their first time out their instructor would take them to a *milonga* where he would ask a woman friend to dance with the novice. I imagined the music snaking through a blue haze of cigarette smoke, sweat and pheromones as the women assessed the men whose hands were upon them. If the novice *tanguero* wasn't good enough he would have to go back to the *practicas* for months more of practice, patience and frustration.

I was struck by the psychology of the tango, that by learning the woman's role as follower the man could develop the empathy that would give a woman the confidence to be led by him in a dance in which nothing is set and there are no words. Reflecting on my marriage I thought it might have worked out better if I had been able to empathise with Mimi more than I had. I tried to imagine us learning the tango together but it would have brought out the worst in both of us very quickly.

The contents of the CD were almost poetic, with such titles as 'The Hunger of the Soul for Contact with Another Soul'. After a while I reached 'Before the Embrace' and from there I went to 'The Hold' with its overhead diagram of two upper bodies heart to heart. I thought of myself and Barbara Strozzi, bosoms touching, heart to heart. Then came the animated footsteps forward and back, this way and that, giving me the eerie sensation of looking up through a glass floor at disembodied feet. The video showed the legs and feet of leader and follower, going through their steps as often as I clicked on *rewind*. It was difficult to practise the steps while sitting at the computer and watching the monitor screen so I sent away for a set of three CDs in which Christy Cote and and George Garcia, appearing full-length, would show me how to dance the Argentine tango. It was a treat to watch them: Christy, smiling all the time, and George, smiling less, made everything wonderfully clear, and I did the lessons in front of the TV with the remote control in hand to repeat and pause the action as necessary as they took me through the Embrace, the *Basico*, the *Cambio de Peso en el Lugar*, the *Paso al Costado*, the *Cadencia*, the *Caminada*, and so on down the line. That was all very well as far as it went but doing it alone was not giving me much satisfaction. I was learning the names of the steps and how they looked when danced by professionals but I knew I wasn't actually going to be learning tango until I had a partner to embrace.

So it was that on a Saturday evening in May I found myself on a Circle Line train watching the stops unreel towards Farringdon. The carriage was full of young people and vernal expectation but I am a November sort of person, and I thought of the big rain that always comes in November to leave the trees black and bare next morning and the ground covered with brown leaves. I'm only forty but I've got November inside me with grey skies, rain, brown leaves and bare black trees.

The Circle Line is some kind of metaphor: from South Kensington you can get to Farringdon eastbound via Victoria and Embankment on the lower part of the loop or you can do it westbound via Paddington and King's Cross on the upper part of the loop. I took it eastbound.

My Underground book was *The Dybbuk*, a play by S. Ansky. In it Leah says, 'If one of us dies before his time, his soul returns to the world to complete its span, to do the things left undone and experience the happiness and griefs he would have known.' Barbara Strozzi died at fifty-eight in Padua in 1677. Had she left things undone, had she had enough happiness and griefs? In Google I found a Barbara Strozzi site where I learned that, although some have theorised that she was a courtesan, this, despite the look of the portrait, seems unlikely. She had four children, three of them with Giovanni Paolo Vidman. They never married but he provided dowries for two of their daughters to enter a convent and an inheritance for one son; the other became a monk. Barbara Strozzi left a body of work that is widely performed by recording artists but I have never seen notices for a live concert. She never gained the patronage she hoped for. And yet! such is the aura of this woman that something of her travelled with me on the Circle Line.

At Victoria three young women got on the train and began to speak Swedish to one another. One of them, a blonde with long straight hair, was a beauty; she couldn't help knowing it and her awareness of it showed in the beautiful way she turned to speak to her companions or inclined her head to listen. They got off the train at Westminster, the beauty leaving a phantom self behind.

I was going to EC1, to St James's Church, Clerkenwell. I'd never been to that part of town before, it seemed remote and dangerous. Might I fall off the edge of the world? Might there be wyverns, cockatrices, anthropophagi, muggers? Was it wise to go there with Pluto coming over my Sagittarian ascendant?

From Liverpool Street onward I was alone in the carriage. Why was no one else going where I was going? Moorgate appeared, Barbican, then there was Farringdon. The station, which was also a main line station, was glass-roofed, like the old Fulham Broadway. Through the glass came dimnesses of yellow light. I looked for a sign of some kind, a favouring omen however modest. FOUND, said a Yahoo ad on the wall opposite. OK, I could work with that.

Outside the station stood a newsvendor at his kiosk. OCKERMAN UNDER INVESTIGATION was the headline on display. I'm used to this; I looked away, then looked again and the word was DONORS. Clerkenwell was full of darkness; the street lamps did what they could but were overwhelmed. Behind the newsvendor, on the opposite side of the street, a cluster of lights and colour offered FOOD & WINE, also Fruit & Veg, which were arrayed under little canopies out on the pavement. To the right was the Bagel Factory: The American Original. To the left, a doorway called Chariots displayed a telephone number and was evidently a minicab stand. Four young men stood waiting there as when the curtain goes up on the first act of a play. I was in Cowcross Street but there were no cows crossing.

Going left, I reached the corner of Turnmill Street. golden gleamings in the dark. Next to it as I entered Turnmill was Pret A Manger with sushi and espresso, then Ember, looking warm and with a large menu on the pavement.

Leaving the zone of conviviality I was on the left-hand side of the street. Below me on my left was the long shape of the main-line station showing dim blind lights as I was swallowed up in the visible darkness. 'The moon's my constant Mistrisse,' I sang tunelessly to the colours in my mind,

> And the lowlie owle my morrowe,
> The flaming Drake and the Nightcrowe make
> Mee musicke to my sorrowe.

There was no moon.

Turnmill Street was tumultuous with silence, as if only a moment ago there had been voices, laughter and music not of this time. On the opposite side was Benjamin Street but I saw no left-handed slingers. Turk's Head Yard was knot a problem. Brown leaves always. Slightly downhill on Turnmill became slightly uphill as I neared Clerkenwell Road. Turned right into Clerkenwell Road, then crossed into Clerkenwell Close where the Crown Tavern beckoned but I carried on and around a dark corner and there was St James's Church, high above the rest of London, its spire aimed at the night sky where planets were approaching new alignments.

Over the road the Three Kings pub glowed cosily. The church was dark; the iron gates on the steps were open. Barbara Strozzi had been with me in the Underground and she was with me even more strongly now. The air is full of all kinds of signals, from the ghostly voices and laughter in Turnmill Street to the more powerful Strozzi presence; the people may be gone but some essence of them remains to travel where it will, unfettered by limitations of time and space. Certainly it's a long time and a long way from Strozzi's Venice to London, but if Venice can reach London by short wave and satellite, why shouldn't the Barbara Strozzi signal also bounce off the ionosphere and the atmosphere to get here?

I went a little way up the main stairs, then down the well-lit steps to the crypt. The door stood open, brightness inside. Please, I said to myself, let it happen. What? I didn't know. A smiling Japanese woman was sitting at a table collecting the admission fee. I paid my eight pounds and crossed the floor to where there were tables and chairs.

The crypt looked festive. The vaulted brick ceiling was partly yellow and partly red in the lighting from below. Other lights were garlanded around the walls and a large round clock hung over the centre of the dance floor. There was a table for tea, coffee, biscuits and soft drinks, with a price list and a tin for collecting coins. The place was gradually filling up with people, a murmur of voices and a quiet party atmosphere. I bought myself a tea and a couple of biscuits, sat down at a table and looked around.

I saw a woman bringing a cup of tea or coffee to a nearby table; she was about five foot nine, very well set-up, and of a commanding presence. Early, maybe mid-thirties I thought. Black T-shirt under a green velvet jacket, short denim skirt, purple tights, black boots, exemplary legs. Before sitting down she stared directly at me. What are *you* looking at? said her eyes. A long oval face with a sullen mouth and an up-yours expression. But attractive, a face that pulled the eye. Dark hair piled up in a way that was defiantly out of date. A Barbara Strozzi, yes, a Barbara Strozzi kind of look. I didn't get where I am today by refraining from making a fool of myself, so I went over to her and said, 'Hi.'

'OK,' she said. 'Now what?'

'You sound suspicious,' I said.

'I am. That's what happens after a certain number of Saturday nights.'

'Should I try again on Monday?'

'Give up easily, do you?'

'Not ordinarily but I'm full of uncertainty; tonight isn't like other nights.'

'What, is it Passover or something?'

'I'll explain later. I'm Phil Ockerman.'

'Bertha Strunk.'

'Is Bertha's trunk anything like Pandora's box?'

'That isn't something you can find out in five minutes.'

'I've got all the time in the world.'

'People say that but you never really do know how much time you have. Anyhow, Phil, it takes two to tango.'

'Well, Bertha, that's what we're here for, isn't it?' My desire was inflamed by her use of my name.

She reached for the book that was sticking out of my pocket. 'What's a dybbuk?' she said. She pronounced it correctly.

'A dybbuk,' I said, 'is the soul of a dead person that, "finding neither rest nor harbour", enters the body of a living person and takes control.'

'Why?'

'Various kinds of unfinished business. In this play it was love.'

She gave me a serious look. 'Do you believe in dybbuks?'

'I believe more things all the time, so right now I'd say that I do believe in dybbuks. Do you?'

'I'll have to wait and see.'

The room was filling up, there were at least fifty people here by now, young, middle-aged and old in all shapes and sizes. In a few minutes the class would start but I didn't want our conversation to stop. 'Bertha,' I said, 'what kind of work do you do?'

'I paint artificial eyes.'

'You do paintings of them?'

'No, I paint the actual plastic eye that goes into the eye socket.'

'Unusual occupation. How did you get into it?'

'I had a friend who lost an eye and the making of his artificial eye got me interested in that kind of work.'

I imagined a man with his real eye looking to the left or right and his artificial one looking straight ahead and I asked Bertha about that.

'Both eyes move together,' she said. 'The artificial one is attached to the muscles of the eye socket. That's enough about me for now. What about you? What do you do?'

'I'm a writer.'

'What do you write?'

'Novels.'

'What's the most recent one?'

'*Hope of a Tree*, just out two months ago.'

'It's not one I've heard of.'

'What's the last thing you've read?'

'*The Da Vinci Code*.'

'Sorry I asked.'

'Actually the writing wasn't very good.'

'Thanks, it's kind of you to say so.'

'Do you make a living with your novels?'

'No, I have to teach as well.'

She nodded as if she hadn't expected me to be a commercial success. Was my unsuccessfulness so apparent?

'Why do you want to learn the tango?' she asked with her head a little to one side.

'I came here looking for someone.'

15

Again she nodded. 'Who?'

'That's a long story.'

'I haven't got all the time in the world but I'll listen if you want to tell me about it.' Was she just being polite?

'I thought you'd never ask,' I said. 'It could be that we have a lot to talk about.'

'Maybe.' With a half-smile.

By now people were making their way to the dance floor for the beginners' class. Michiko Okasaki, the woman who'd been taking the money at the door, and her partner Paul Lange now came to the centre of the floor to start the lesson. She was short, he was tall. All of us beginners stood around them while they demonstrated and explained the embrace, which they called the hold. Next they showed us how the leader walks forward and the follower walks backwards. We learners, without music, took our partners and tried this.

Feeling for the first time Bertha's right hand in my left and the warmth and solidity of her body under my right I could hardly believe what was happening: I was *leading* this woman and she was *following* me. Then she led and I followed, meeting her eyes with mine.

There was a CD player on a table in a corner of the floor, and Paul Lange went to it and started 'La Cumparsita'. It was the same recording I had at home, *Juan D'Arienzo y su Orquesta Tipica*. Surely a sign, surely a good omen, that? The lesson continued with music and moved on to side steps for which we briefly exchanged partners. Instead of holding Bertha I had a chic executive type and we both smiled but I was relieved when I was holding Bertha again for steps outside the partner. The teaching was marvellous, everything was made so easy that I thought I might eventually be capable of real tango dancing. I tried to take my mind back to Barbara Strozzi but all I could think of was Bertha; it was as if an electric current connected the centre of me to the centre of her. As each step was shown us we learners stood and watched and while watching I still held Bertha's hand.

'You've still got my hand,' she said.

'I know,' I said, but I didn't let go and she smiled. High above us the spire aimed itself at the night sky and the restless planets; in the church we stepped forward and back. Under us flowed unseen springs and rivers. I sent my thoughts to Bertha without speaking. I squeezed her hand and she sqeezed back.

We left at the end of the beginners' class. When we turned into Turnmill Street we looked down towards Cowcross. High up we were, looking down on distant lights: a moment that is still with me, flickering always in the changing colours of my mind. We didn't speak at all but there was no ghostly silence this time; there were the voices of other pedestrians and the sound of taxis passing us as we came down Turnmill. There was a hot-dog vendor at the corner by the station. The smell became an unforgettable tune, 'When My Hot Dog Smiles at Me' or whatever, and we hungered for the rolls, the mustard, and the steaming sausages on the cart.

'*Bon appetit*,' said the hot-dog man and we ate them standing on the pavement like two detectives in a cop film.

Bertha lived in Fulham, in the North End Road. My flat was also in Fulham, in Basuto Road, so we both took the Circle Line westbound. We sat down and looked at each other for a few moments as the train left Farringdon. I was expecting the usual exchange of personal histories and provenances, but no: 'How tall are you?' said Bertha.

'How tall am I?' I said, sitting up straighter.

'That's what I said,' said Bertha.

'Five seven,' I said, stretching my neck.

'I'm five nine,' said Bertha.

'So do you want to throw me back or what?'

'I don't know – I'm kind of old-fashioned,' she said after a pause.

'Meaning?'

She blushed, half-shrugged, half-smiled, looked apologetic. 'I want a man who can protect me.'

It was my turn to blush. 'Should I forget tango and take up karate?'

She didn't laugh. 'I'll have to think about this,' she said.

'I'm really confused, Bertha.'

'Me too.'

'I thought there was something happening between us.'

Again the apologetic look, the half-shrug and a little shake of the head. 'Yes and no,' she said.

'Is there some particular thing or person you want protection from?'

'Let's talk about something else,' she said. 'Where are you from?'

'Pennsylvania,' I said lamely. As we travelled west the metaphor of the Circle Line was closing its loop and I felt myself on the outside looking in. She was from Exeter and we pushed these and other counters towards each other while long silences sprang up like brambles. At Paddington we sat saying nothing and looking at the people waiting on the opposite platform until a Wimbledon train arrived. We sat among Saturday-night faces and voices until Fulham Broadway appeared and we got out. I walked her to the North End Road which was full of Saturday-night noise, people, and rubbish. She opened her street door and I followed her up a flight of stairs to her flat. At her door I didn't feel free to kiss her or even take her hand; by then the colours had gone out of the night and everything was like a not-very-good print of a black-and-white film. I just stood there and waited for her to say something. Only a little while ago I had held her, felt the weight and warmth of her body under my hands!

'Give me your phone number,' she said.

I wrote it down on the back of a handbill from the tango class and gave it to her. 'Are you going to give me yours?' I said.

She wrote it on the same handbill, tore off that piece and gave it to me. 'Not too soon,' she said, 'OK?' And I thought that was the end of it for now but as she turned to go inside she paused and turned back to me again. 'Would you like to come in for a coffee?' she said.

'What *is* this?' I said. 'What the hell are you playing at?'

She didn't blush but she shook her head the way one does when baffled. 'Nothing is simple for me,' she said.

'That makes two of us. When I sit down for the coffee, will you pull the chair away or what?'

'I promise not to pull the chair away.' She opened the door. 'Are you going to come in?'

I went in cautiously. There was a smell of rug shampoo. She switched on a light and the flat sprang into view not looking like her. 'This flat belongs to a friend,' she said as she hung our coats on a clothestree by the door.

'Man or woman?'

'Woman,' she said as I followed her into the kitchen. The light was hard, the walls were blue, there was a framed photograph of Sir Cliff Richard. There was a framed print of Jesus with his Sacred Heart exposed. There was a cutesy spice rack, there were smiley magnets on the fridge door.

'Why Cliff Richard?' I said.

'Hilary's doing an Alpha course because he recommended it on the website,' said Bertha. 'This is her kitchen. We've been flatmates for more than a year but I don't put anything of mine on the walls except in my room.'

'You moved here when you broke up with some-body?'

'Yes.'

'Are you with anyone now?'

'No. Are you?'

'No. I was divorced six months ago.'

'Your idea or hers?'

'Hers. She said I was a failure. What about *your* somebody?'

There was a pause while she spooned instant coffee into two mugs, filled the kettle and turned on the gas. I wasn't sure if she'd answer me.

'I left him,' she said. 'We're still married.' Her face now seemed very vulnerable. She took off the velvet jacket and I saw purple bruises symmetrically on both arms as if she had been held and shaken.

'I guess he's more than five nine,' I said.

She nodded.

'Those bruises,' I said, 'are less than a month old.'

She nodded again and crossed her arms to cover them.

'Have you seen *The Rainmaker*?' I said.

'No. Why?'

'In this film a husband's beatings put his wife into hospital. Her name is Kelly. She falls in love with a lawyer called Rudy. When the husband discovers them together he goes for Rudy with a baseball bat. Rudy gets the better of him and beats him half to death. Then Kelly takes the bat and says to Rudy, "Stop! Give me the bat. You were not here tonight. Go!" When he's gone she finishes the job but she beats a murder rap because it was self-defence and no jury would convict her.'

'What happened then?' said Bertha.

'Rudy and the widow go off together and start a new life.'

Bertha poured the coffee and we sat down at the kitchen table while Jesus watched with a shit–happens look on his face. 'Do you think they could?' she said.

'Start a new life?' I could feel Pluto going over my Sagittarian ascendant. Where to?

'Yes,' said Bertha. Her face was soft and she was looking at me as if I might be five foot eight. What a sweet face.

'Certainly,' I said. 'That husband got what was coming to him. Their consciences would be perfectly clear. You ever think of a baseball–bat sort of solution for your problem?'

'Not with a bat.'

'So you *have* thought of it. How would you do it?'

'I *wouldn't* do it. People have fantasies about all kinds of things. How did we get into this anyhow?'

'Your bruises.'

She put on the velvet jacket again. 'Now it's colder in here. Let's take our coffee to my room.'

We went through the sitting room quickly. There was a painting on black velvet of a Spanish dancer. The last time I saw a painting on black velvet was in my grandmother's house in Philadelphia. There was a little shelf of paperbacks; I saw the names of Georgette Heyer and Barbara Cartland. There was a book on the coffee table, *The God That Changes Lives*. There was a little shelf of little glass animals. 'Are you good friends with Hilary?' I said.

'We get on well enough but we don't have much to do with each other. Here's my room.'

The first thing I noticed was a poster of the painting called *Hope*, a young woman in clinging garments sitting on half a globe with her left ankle tucked under her right leg. Her eyes are half-closed as she leans her head against the lyre that she strokes with her right hand. There's a dreamy smile on her face – she looks as if she's stoned out of her mind. I don't know who painted that picture. Where do I remember it from? Was it hanging on a schoolroom wall? Not at the front with George Washington but perhaps in a lesser position at the back. 'Our father who art in heaven,' we said in the morning, 'Hallowed be thy name.' And so on while the planets seen or unseen moved above us. We pledged allegiance to the flag and we sang 'Long, Long Ago' and 'The Little Brown Church in the Vale' and other primary-school standards and then we started our lessons.

'Are you hopeful?' I said.

'I hope that nothing bad is coming my way. What about you?'

'I hope I'll get an idea for a new novel. Do you think he's coming your way?'

23

'Who?' said Bertha.

'Who else? The bruiser, your husband.'

'He knows where I am but I don't think he'll come here. He only gets physical when there aren't any witnesses. If he sees me when there are he doesn't even raise his voice to me. The bruises are from a couple of weeks ago when he caught me in a dark side street with no one about. He gave me a shaking but I got away from him.'

'It's only a matter of time though, isn't it?'

'Everything's a matter of time.' She went to the CD player and put on Marianne Faithfull with the song from the ending of *The Girl on the Bridge*:

> Who will take your dreams away
> Takes your soul another day . . .

Slow and mournful, the words hung in the air between us.

'Not really a happy song,' I said.

'The dreams I have, I'd be glad for them to be taken away,' said Bertha. She stopped the recording.

More and more I was feeling that she wanted something from me. What brings people together at a particular place and time? 'How did you find out about the crypt at St James's?' I said.

'Girl I know told me about it. Something else – when I heard the name of the church I got a picture in my mind.'

'Of what?'

'A yahoo ad on a wall with the word FOUND. I took that as a sign.'

'Which it is. On the wall at Farringdon.'

'You know what I mean – I took it as a sign that I'd found the right place.'

'The right place for what?'

'Something more than a tango lesson.'

I was watching her face for any indication that I might be that something. Maybe the hint of the beginning of a smile. 'Don't ask too many questions,' she said. 'It's unlucky. You were going to explain why this night was different from other nights for you.'

'I came to St James's looking for Barbara Strozzi,' I said.

She gave me a hard look. 'Who's Barbara Strozzi?'

I told her all there was to tell, including my sensing of Strozzi's presence in the Underground and at the Clerkenwell church. 'Does that sound crazy to you?'

'Yes, but crazy is OK sometimes – you have to trust what pulls you. If you want to go where it's pulling you.'

All during this conversation I could feel the fragile architecture of trust and comradeship building up between us. The wrong word, the wrong move, would make it collapse like a house of cards. I drank my coffee and looked at *Hope*. 'Shall I say more about Barbara Strozzi?' I said.

'Yes.'

'When I saw you I saw Barbara Strozzi in you. Her music brought me to the tango but seeing you took me back to her music, her *cantate* and *lamentate*.'

'You're a pretty weird guy, aren't you.'

'Yes, you might as well know that right from the start.'

She looked at me for a while as if she was deciding whether to go along with the weirdness or back away from it. I could see myself coming up full-screen and then minimising in her eyes as she clicked her mental mouse. 'I'll have to listen to her music some time,' she said.

'How about now?' I said.

'You came prepared.'

'I have my little CD player and a Strozzi disc with me because I thought I might listen to it in the train.' The disc was *Diporti di Euterpe*, with Emanuela Galli, Ensemble Galilei and Paul Beier. I ejected Marianne Faithfull and inserted Strozzi.

Bertha was looking at the CD brochure with the lyrics which also had a black-and-white reproduction of the Strozzi portrait in the Royal Academy exhibition. 'Actually,' she said, 'there *is* a resemblance. Mostly it's the look on her face. I see that same look every day in the mirror.'

'Here she comes,' I said. The first track was '*Tradimento*'. 'Betrayal'. Bertha said nothing for a few moments as Galli's voice spun into the room over the baroque guitars backing it. Then, 'That certainly sounds like another time and place. I don't quite see how you found your way from this to tango music.' She picked up the translation. 'Cupid and Hope want to take me prisoner . . .' she read out. She stood shaking her head as she turned towards me. 'Cupid,' she said. 'Hope. Betrayal.'

I took her by both bruised arms and pulled her to me and kissed her. She kept her mouth closed for a moment, then opened it as we pressed against each other. She tasted like peaches and cream, like summer and sunshine, like hope. Thank you, I said to the wheeling stars and unseen planets high above us in the night.

That was as far as it went that night. We didn't end up in bed. When I left her I spun out into the North End Road where the street lamps glowed like fire balloons. A 28 bus trundled by as shiny and sweetly red as a toffee apple. Scatterings of Saturday-night shouted and screamed in random decibels that spiralled into the darkness above the illuminations of Ryman, Fish and Chips, and Cancer Research UK. Brightness pervaded the North End Road all the way to the night lights in Waitrose. At the roundabout I crossed to the Fulham Road which was awash with buses, cars, taxis, litter and louts of all classes. Turned into Barclay Road at Domino's Pizza and made my way to the west side of Eel Brook Common, Basuto Road and home, descending through levels of unlight and quiet to ordinary reality where I was uncertain of her kiss that still lingered on my tongue.

My flat looked different now; it seemed pleased with what I was bringing to it. I poured myself a Glenfiddich, said, 'Here's looking at you,' and sat down to try to remember Bertha's face. I could hear her voice but her face wouldn't come.

Nicely warmed by the whisky, I got *Maps of the Heavens* off the shelf where it lay – it's too tall to stand up – and turned to Albrecht Dürer's marvellous sixteenth-century woodcut of the northern celestial hemisphere. There was Sagittarius the centaur aiming his arrow at Scorpio; I could feel the vibration of his bowstring but I couldn't find Pluto; maybe he was busy in the underworld. That's how it is – you can't always see what's going on.

I dialled Bertha. 'What?' she said.

'It's me,' I said. I noticed that I had put my hand on my heart.

'I know,' she said.

'Would you tell me your birth date, time of birth, and place of birth? I want to ask my astrologer to do your horoscope.'

'You have a personal astrologer?'

'The same as I have a GP and a dentist,' I said. 'I'm not her only client.'

'You want my horoscope because . . .?'

'Because whatever this is we're in, we're in it to-gether so it's a good idea to know how the stars and planets are for both of us. Don't you think?'

There was a pause at her end. Then, 'I don't want to know too much.'

'Because it would . . .?'

'Get in the way of whatever I might be doing. I'd fall down stairs, slip on banana skins, get run over by buses, walk into plate-glass doors – that kind of thing.'

'How about if I get your horoscope and don't tell you anything, keep it all to myself?'

'Then I'd catch you looking at me in a certain way and I'd think, oh shit, what has he found out about my stars? No, it's a bad idea.'

'OK. When can I see you again?'

'You're not tired of me yet? I'm a lot of trouble.'

'It's a lot of trouble *not* seeing you.'

'I think we both need a little time to settle down. Can you phone me Thursday?'

'OK, Thursday.'

'And when you phone, call me Barbara – that way I'll always know it's you.'

'Barbara.'

'Yes, Phil.'

'Till Thursday, then, Barbara.'

'Till Thursday, Phil.'

We rang off and I poured myself another drink. The phone rang.

'Barbara?' I said.

'I was born on 17 August 1967,' she said. 'In Exeter. At quarter to nine in the morning.'

'You changed your mind about horoscopes!'

'Yes, I'm tired of being afraid of everything. Show it

to me when you get it, I want to know all there is to know.'

I e-mailed her details to Catriona. Then I went online and ordered a personalised baseball bat from the Louisville Slugger gift shop in Louisville, Kentucky. The Boston Red Sox won the 2004 World Series, so this bat would have the Red Sox logo plus the engraving, in three lines:

GENUINE
Barbara Strozzi
LOUISVILLE SLUGGER

It would take a couple of weeks to get here.

While waiting for the bat to arrive I'd be seeing Bertha (Bertha/Barbara) whenever possible, teaching my classes, and cruising for Page One. Until now I'd always put events of my own life into my novels. This time I wasn't going to do that; whatever was happening with Bertha/Barbara and me would be kept separate from my writing.

2

BERTHA/BARBARA STRUNK

Here I am again, getting into something I'll probably be sorry for. As always. What else can I do – lock myself up to keep from making mistakes? Why did I tell Phil to call me Barbara? There *is* something between me and Barbara Strozzi. What it is I don't know. BS also means bullshit. Why did I kiss him the way I did? I guess I need to have a man wanting me. Pathetic.

He left the CD with me, and after he'd gone I put it on and listened to it for a while but I couldn't really get with it. The singer sounded either fretful or miserable or both; she sounded like a victim, which is not what I am. Although I make a lot of mistakes. With men mostly. Both short and tall.

Professor Adderley is a good example of what I'm talking about. He taught drawing and painting at Humberside University and he also lectured on Art History. A big man, tall and broad with a beard. In his forties. He was very free with his hands and he liked to invite girls to his studio for private sessions. He was looking over my shoulder one day when I was painting a costume model, a girl in a flapper dress. 'You're missing the essence of flapper,' he said. 'Flapper is free and easy but your painting is tight. You need to loosen up.' I said I'd try. He had whisky on his breath. Later he stopped me in the hall and said, 'You have a very good walk. If you could paint like you walk there'd be a big improvement in your work.'

I said, 'Thanks, I'll keep that in mind.' I had a pretty good idea what was coming next. One evening he caught me coming out of the Union bar with a couple of pints in me and he breathed on me and said, 'I'd like to paint you. Would you pose for me?'

Some of his paintings were hanging in the halls – they were harsh and raw, with garish colours, something like John Bratby. I was curious to see how I'd look in a painting by him so I said, 'OK. With my clothes on, right?'

'Any way you like,' he said. This was on a Monday and I agreed to come to his studio on Saturday. On Tuesday he did a lecture with slides on Caravaggio, Carracci, Gentileschi, and other fifteenth-century Roman painters. Orazio Gentileschi had a daughter, Artemisia, who was the first woman to paint historical and religious subjects. One of the slides was her *Judith Slaying Holofernes*. 'Very strong,' said Professor Adderley. 'She learned a lot from Caravaggio. But the power in this picture comes from her own experience. She'd been studying with Agostino Tassi and he raped her. So she cut off his head in this picture and her rage made it one of the best things she ever did. She enjoyed it so much she did a second version, with Holofernes's leg visible as he struggles while the maidservant holds him down. Did two more with Judith and the maidservant sneaking out with the head – all four paintings first-rate.'

On Saturday I went to Prof. Adderley's place. Middle of May but grey and rainy. Rode there on my bike with Marianne Faithfull in my head, singing:

At the age of thirty-seven she realised she'd never
Ride through Paris in a sports car with the warm
    wind in her hair,
So she let the phone keep ringing as she sat there
    softly singing
Pretty nursery rhymes she'd memorised in her
    daddy's easy chair . . .

Prof. Adderley had a house in town. Wife and two kids. The studio was a separate little building in the back. It looked like his home away from home: there were a skylight and a north-light window, a galley, a well-stocked bar, a fridge full of beer, and a sleeping alcove.

'It's not all that warm in here,' he said. 'Can I offer you something to take the chill off? A little Courvoisier maybe?'

'Why not?' I said.

He poured me a fairly large one and one for himself. 'Here's to Art and all who sail in her,' he said, and we clinked glasses. 'I'll do some sketches first,' he said. 'See where it takes us.' I was wearing jeans and a pullover. So he sketched for a while, then he shook his head and said, 'Really, a body like yours, it's a shame to cover it up. Plus I think that taking your clothes off would free you up generally.'

I could see what was going on in his head as if it were a video, and right there was where I should have put a stop to the whole thing but I didn't. I thought I looked pretty good with no clothes on, and, as Zero Mostel said in *The Producers*, 'If ya got it, flaunt it.' So I flaunted it, stupid me. Prof. Adderley ('Please, call me Brian') gave me a kimono and a screen to change behind, then when I came out and took off the kimono he studied me from various angles before arranging me on some cushions. Setting the pose required a lot of handling and his hands tended to linger wherever he put them. Next thing I knew he'd unzipped his trousers and was on top of me. A heavy man, and strong.

'Stop!' I said. 'Put your Agostino Tassi back in your pants!'

'Come on, Bertha,' he said. 'This can't be that much of a surprise to you.'

'You're the one that'll get a surprise if you don't get off me,' I said. There was a serious struggle, then I punched him and bit and scratched, I was in a real rage, as much at myself for being stupid as at him for trying to rape me. I was fighting as hard as I could, and without meaning to I jabbed my thumb into his left eye. Hard. He screamed and jumped up, and there was the eye half-hanging out of his head and blood pouring down his face. 'You bitch!' he said, trying to put the eye back where it belonged. 'Get me an ambulance!'

I dialled 999 and hurried into my clothes but before the ambulance and his wife came I took his mahlstick – it was an aluminium one with a rubber ball on the end – and rolled it over his face to get blood on it.

'What the hell are you doing?' he yelled.

'You had the mahlstick in your hand when you tripped over something and that's how it happened,' I said.

'That's odd,' his wife said when she burst into the studio. She looked at the blank canvas and then at me. 'He doesn't ordinarily use a mahlstick at this stage,' she said. He was moaning and groaning and cursing. 'You never were very good at nudes,' she said to him. 'This one must have given you a lot of trouble.' She was a good-looking brunette about twenty years younger than Adderley.

'You're a real comfort to me,' he said. 'Maybe you could get me a drink.'

She poured him a cognac and one for herself and stood looking at him while she drank it.

The paramedics arrived then. 'Jesus!' said one of them to Adderley. 'What happened?'

He showed them the mahlstick. 'Got this in my eye,' he said. 'Hurts like hell.'

They gave him painkillers but they didn't seem to help much. When they put him in the ambulance his wife gave me a hard look and said, 'Why don't you go along and hold his hand – I'm stuck here with the kids.'

All the way to the hospital he held on to my hand. One of the paramedics was with us while the other one drove, so the Prof. didn't say anything to me but he squeezed my hand and mouthed the words, '*Please forgive me.*'

'*It's OK,*' I mouthed back. '*I'm sorry I hurt you.*' I was, too.

At the hospital they examined him in A & E and sent him up to surgery to have the eye removed. When he was out of surgery I sat by his bed and waited for him to come out of the anaesthetic. After a while he put his hand up to the bandages and felt around, then he opened his one eye. 'I'm glad I've still got one eye to see you with,' he said.

I said, 'I'm glad you're glad.' I didn't know what else to say. He seemed humbled by what had happened. I took his hand and said, 'When you're ready to go back to work I'll pose for you again if you want me to.'

'I do,' he said. 'Looking at you made me want to paint in a new way. I don't want to do ugly any more.' He closed his eye and went to sleep then and I got a minicab back to his place for my bike. It was dark by then. His wife came to the door when she heard the car. She didn't say anything, just stood there with the light behind her. Then she closed the door and I rode home with Marianne Faithfull and 'The Ballad of Lucy Jordan' in my head again.

Brian was back at work in a week with his eye still bandaged and he said his wife had left him and taken the kids. He didn't seem to be exactly broken up about it; he told me this was the second wife who'd left him. He had visitation rights for the daughter of the first marriage, now a teenager, and he expected the same for the little son and daughter of the second. I had the feeling that he wasn't up for a lot of quality time with his kids.

He wanted me to pose again so I did. When I came out from behind the screen I dropped the kimono and we stood looking at each other.

'What?' he said.

'Here I am,' I said. 'I owe you one.' I didn't know I was going to say that. Then again, I think I did. And that was how I became Brian Adderley's mistress. He turned out to be not such a bad guy, or maybe I turned out to be not such a good girl. His new paintings were a whole lot better than the old ones, they were less about him and more about what he was looking at. Which was me most of the time. We drank a lot of cognac and beer and we ate a lot of pizza, Chinese, Thai and Indian take-aways. I put on a few pounds which quite pleased Brian. 'The more of you, the better,' he said. His new paintings were better – more sensitive than the earlier ones. I couldn't help being proud of that.

When they removed Brian's eye in hospital the surgeon inserted an implant made of coral compound which was attached to the eye muscles so that it could move naturally. It took four weeks for this to heal, then we went to London and stayed at the Regent Palace Hotel for the two days it took to make the artificial eye.

The ocularists were two brothers, Karl and Georg (pronounced Gayorg) Lichtheim, who had a studio in Berwick Street. Both of them were tall and thin with grey hair. Karl did all the steps up to the painting, then Georg painted the eye and put in the little red threads for the veins.

The room where they worked was big and bright and looked something like a dentist's surgery. Equipment everywhere. Charts on the walls and diplomas from Germany. First they took an impression of the eye socket and made a mould. Then from the mould they made a wax shell which was carved and fitted. The iris button was inserted in this and the position checked for accuracy when the eye moved. From this they cast the plastic shape which would be the finished eye. This was ground down and a temporary plastic shell made. Then the eye was painted and clear plastic was processed over the paint.

So there we were then. We went back to Humberside and it was business and pleasure as usual. Brian still had an eye for the girls but I was the only one that ever was invited to the studio. Even if he'd had others I wouldn't have minded – it was an OK arrangement while I finished the course but I wasn't in love with him. He had proprietary feelings about me and tried to convince me that I could become a better painter. 'I've changed because of what happened between us,' he said. 'That experience has been absorbed into my painting and you should make use of it in yours.'

He liked to talk about Artemisia Gentileschi. Probably he had fantasies of her when he was in bed with me. He bought a book about her and one about her and her father, Orazio. He was dead keen on Artemisia's *Judith Slaying Holofernes*. I believe he'd have liked to be dominated by a woman like that Judith. 'Look at the arms on her!' he used to say. 'She didn't need the sword for the job, she could have torn his head off with her bare hands. And look at this one with Judith and the maidservant sneaking out with the head in a basket, how the hand she holds up to block the light of the candle throws a shadow on her face like a death-cloud. And notice that she's still got the sword – she's ready for anything. What a woman!'

'Judith or Artemisia?' I said.

'Both.' He opened the other book. 'Look here,' he said, 'this is Orazio's *Rest on the Flight to Egypt*, with Joseph having a kip while Baby Jesus has a pint or so of Mary's Best. Nobody does a better Jesus on the tit than Orazio. Look at Mary's sweet expression and the dreamy sensuality in the eye of Baby Jesus. Absolutely first-rate. Now let's see what Orazio does with Judith and Holofernes. He seems to have avoided the scene where she tops him – a little too rich for his blood maybe. The closest he gets is Judith with Abra, her maidservant, and the head. The head is like a hired prop and the whole thing, which is necessarily posed, *looks* posed, as if he's told his two female models, "Pretend you've just heard something and you're scared." So Judith looks up as if she's just heard a pizza delivery at the door and Abra isn't sure whether she's heard anything or not. Orazio just didn't have the balls for Judith.'

'Maybe *you'd* like to do Judith and Holofernes,' I said to Brian.

'I might just have a go at that,' he said. 'You'll be Judith and I'll be Holofernes.'

'Whatever turns you on,' I said. So we did Judith and Holofernes. I posed for Judith and the maidservant and I photographed Brian in the Holofernes pose and costume. He painted two pictures. In the first one Holofernes is in white tie and wearing all his medals. He's leaning back against Judith with his left hand between her legs while she garrots him with a white silk scarf. She's wearing diamonds and she's more out of than in a strapless white satin sheath. Abra, the maidservant, is naked except for white stockings as she kneels in front of Holofernes embracing his legs and looking up at his last moments.

The second painting is a closer view with Judith and Abra kissing as the maidservant dangles the head by its hair. Both paintings were done in the manner of Artemisia Gentileschi, and Judith had arms like a stevedore. A very striking pair of pictures, both of them over two feet high. It took us three months for the two of them and I stopped counting the hours I posed, the drinks we drank, the takeaways we ate, and the pounds I gained.

Although they were done in a style not his own, there was still something strong and original in those paintings. I'd seen a lot of his work and these were his best. 'Are you going to exhibit them?' I said.

'Where?'

'I don't know anything about the art world. The Royal Academy Summer Exhibition?'

'Wankers,' he said. 'Somebody's going to pay real money for these.'

'Who?'

'I've got one or two connections,' he said. I carried on with my classes and waited to see what would happen. A couple of days later there was a Rolls parked in the drive, a chauffeur having a smoke, and a large lady all in pink in the studio. 'Lady Constance Ullage,' said Brian, 'this is my good friend and model, Bertha Strunk.'

'How do you do,' I said.

'Charmed,' said Lady Constance. She looked me up and down and from several angles, took hold of my chin, turned my face this way and that, and said, 'I am keen to see what he's done with you.' She spoke very posh.

'Perhaps a little something to refresh the critical faculties?' said Brian.

'Gin, please,' said Lady Constance. I poured for her

and she knocked back a couple of quick ones while Brian went to the rack, took out *Judith Slaying Holofernes*, and put it up on the easel. 'Here she is,' he said. 'Twice.'

Lady Constance looked from the painting to me and back again. 'Piquant,' she said.

'And here's the companion piece,' said Brian, '*Judith and Her Maidservant with the Head of Holofernes*.'

'Touching,' said Lady Constance. She patted me on the bottom and said, 'Keep up the good work.' To Brian she said, 'I'll phone you,' and swept out like a pink wedding cake on wheels.

'She looks like real money,' I said.

'She can just about afford the Rolls,' said Brian, 'but she knows seriously rich people.'

There was a phone call the next day from Lady Constance, and the day after that an E–Type pulled up in the drive and a man in a white suit, black shirt, no tie and a panama hat stepped out. When he spoke it was with a South African accent. 'Judith, I presume?' he said, and kissed my hand.

'That's me,' I said.

'I am Theodor von Augenblick. Is Holofernes at home?'

'This way, please,' I said, and led him to the studio. Brian had evidently been briefed by Lady Constance because he took a bottle of apricot schnapps from the fridge and I poured it into little glasses.

'*Prosit!*' said von Augenblick.

'*Prosit!*' said Brian.

'*Prosit!*' said I. Clink, and Brian went to the rack.

Von Augenblick settled himself in the viewing chair while I poured again and *Judith Slaying Holofernes* went up on the easel.

'*Prima!*' said von Augenblick. 'With this kind of thing you don't lose money.'

Up went *Judith and Her Maidservant with the Head of Holofernes*.

'Bravo!' said von Augenblick. 'These will move, that I promise you.' To me he said, 'I can see that you have been a real inspiration. I hope this man appreciates you.'

'I do,' said Brian.

We all had another drink, then von Augenblick said to Brian, 'How long does it take you to do paintings like these?'

'Three months for these two,' said Brian.

'I am well acquainted in Dubai,' said von Augenblick, 'and I believe something could be done there with these and others from your brush. I have in mind variations on this theme: Judith and the maidservant and Holofernes *before* the party was over, and Judith and the maidservant in more intimate situations after. What do you think?' He said this while undressing me with his eyes.

Brian looked from von Augenblick to me and said, ' "When Duty whispers low, *Thou must*, the youth replies, *I can*." '

'This is a youth who will not go hungry,' said von

Augenblick to me. 'Now, if I may abduct these two beauties from the seraglio?'

'They'll be delighted to go with you,' said Brian. He wrapped them up in brown paper and shook hands with von Augenblick who kissed my hand. Then von Augenblick and the two beauties got into the E-Type and roared away.

'Oughtn't you to have got a receipt or something?' I said to Brian.

'You don't do that with people like him,' said Brian. 'Either there's trust or you back away altogether.'

'And you do trust him? He seemed awfully smooth to me.'

'Oh, he's definitely a smoothie but I do trust him, and now let's get to work on dirty pictures.'

So the fridge was restocked and once more the takeaway deliveries started beating a path to our door. I stretched canvases while Brian sketched various compositions and we got into the spirit of the thing pretty quickly. Sometimes, when we tried different poses, one thing led to another and it was a while before work resumed. I have to say it was a fun time, and the thought of a result in Dubai kept us feeling good.

We heard nothing from von Augenblick for three weeks, at the end of which time there arrived a cheque for £266,667 to Brian. The paintings had sold for £500,000. Von Augenblick's 33.33 per cent commission left a balance of £333,333 and Lady Constance's

20 per cent commission came off that. 'Half of this goes to you,' said Brian.

I said, 'I don't want any money from this. You've got two wives and three children to think of.'

'They're already getting regular support,' Brian said, 'and there's more money where this came from. They'll get a big share of the next lot. Don't let's argue about it, we've got work to do.'

We carried on with the second Judith and Holofernes painting which was straight pornography, you couldn't call it anything else. That night I dreamt that I'd ordered pizza, and when I heard a knock on the door I opened it and there was Artemisia Gentileschi. She didn't say anything, just handed me the pizza. When I tried to pay her she shook her head, got back on her motor scooter and roared away. I woke up and there was Brian beside me, snoring and smelling like a distillery. I put my hand up to my face and it didn't feel like my face. I stayed awake for a long time, trying to remember how Artemisia had looked when she handed me the pizza. The box had felt warm so I knew there was a pizza inside but I thought there might be a message as well and I wanted to get back to the dream but I couldn't. Maybe, I thought, what was in the box wasn't a pizza.

Brian was lecturing the next morning and I should have been in class but instead I went to the dean's office. Graduation was only a month away but I said that I was urgently needed at home and asked him if I could complete my course work and deliver it as soon as possible for my degree. He looked at my records and agreed. Then I hurried back to the studio, threw my things into a bag, and went to the bread bin where Brian always kept a lot of cash. I took out £500 which I reckoned he owed me for pre-Dubai posing and inspiration, left a note saying that I didn't want any of the Dubai money and caught a bus to London. I got a room at the Earls Court YMCA and there I was. Sometimes I do things without knowing exactly why I do them. That's one of my problems.

I'd been thinking about artificial eyes. It seemed like a nice neat quiet kind of work and I needed a job. I went to see the Lichtheim brothers in Berwick Street. Karl said, 'This is for you a lucky day. Georg thinks of retiring and we will try whether you can be trained for this work. We begin with two days a week and we see where it goes.'

They started me on irises. That went all right and pretty soon I was working full-time painting artificial eyes. Karl and Georg liked country and western music, and I heard a lot of Hank Williams, Waylon Jennings, Johnny Cash, Patsy Cline and Emmylou Harris while I worked. The song that was most often in my head was Johnny Cash singing 'Sunday Morning Coming Down'.

> On a Sunday morning sidewalk,
> I'm wishin', Lord, that I was stone,
> 'Cause there's somethin' in a Sunday
> That makes a body feel alone . . .

That song was in my head on a Friday evening when I was in Earls Court Road going home. Feeling perfectly safe when all of a sudden I was dragged into a side street. With all those people around! There were two of them, both white, and I didn't know if it was a mugging or rape they had in mind. I fought like a wildcat, and this time I really tried to stick my thumb in somebody's eye but I wasn't doing all that well when – it was like magic – the one holding me from behind wasn't there any more. Next, somebody big got between me and the one in front and he laid that one out with a kick to the chin. Very impressive.

'Thank you,' I said. He was well over six feet. Square-jawed martial-arts hero type.

'My pleasure,' he said. 'Will you let me walk you home?'

'Yes, I will, but what about him?' The one he'd kicked was still out cold and I think he had a broken jaw. The other one had run off.

'What *about* him?' he said. 'That's an occupational hazard in his line of work.'

'Maybe we should call an ambulance.'

'Call one if you want but I won't wait around for it. The paramedics will give the police a bell and there'll be paperwork and I'll probably get done for GBH.'

'OK, I'll just tell the ambulance where to find him and we'll go.' I dialled 999 on my mobile, made my call, and we walked away.

'What's your name?' I asked my new friend.

'Troy Wallis.'

'Unusual name.'

'I'm an unusual guy. And your name?'

'Bertha Strunk.' He smiled a little smile when I said it. 'The boys at school used to make jokes about Bertha's trunk,' I said, 'and I gave them more than one bloody nose. Are you going to make a joke?'

'No. You're very physical, aren't you.'

'I don't know. More than some, less than others, I guess.'

He grabbed me and kissed me, a really serious kiss with a lot of tongue action. I could have kept my mouth closed but I didn't. He moved both hands down to get a good grip on my bottom and we stood like that for a while.

'You're pretty physical yourself,' I said when I got my mouth back. He was still in charge of my bottom.

'I'm a very simple guy – when I see what I want I go for it.'

'Are you going to walk me home or are we just going to stand here and make a pair of spectacles of ourselves?'

'Sorry, kissing you made me lose track of time.' He gave me his arm and we walked.

I guess I'm a very shallow person, really, but it felt good to be with a big strong man who wanted to look after me. That might not be a good enough reason to marry somebody but three months later I was Mrs Troy Wallis. I've just written how it happened but even now I ask myself how in the world it did happen.

He was a bouncer at Jimmy Maloney's in the Fulham Road. He worked nights and I worked days so we didn't see a lot of each other and living with Mr Muscles was pretty boring. We didn't have much to talk about and it's just as well that I'm not in the habit of writing home because the sex was nothing to write home about. It was about a month before he started bouncing me around. I was living in his flat in Harwood Road by then. It happened one evening when I gave him his tea before he left for work. Bangers and mash. No veg, he didn't care much for veg. He looked at it and said, 'What kind of rubbish is this?'

I said, 'Banger rubbish and mash rubbish.'

He said, 'Don't you come it with me, I'm not in the mood.'

'I wouldn't dream of it, I know how sensitive you are.'

'And none of your sarcasm either.'

'Not even a little?'

Wham! He gave me a backhander that broke my nose and sent me flying across the room. 'That's pretty good,' I said. 'How's your forehand?'

'I'm warning you! Watch your mouth before I get mad and knock your teeth down your throat.' With that he threw the bangers and mash on the floor and stomped out.

That was the last evening I spent under Troy Wallis's roof. I packed a bag and went to Chelsea & Westminster Hospital where, after waiting about an hour, I had my nose fixed by a young doctor who wanted to know who'd done that to me. I told him I'd walked into a glass door. I crashed at the Lichtheim studio that night, and the next day I found this flatshare. Troy hassles me in the street sometimes but so far he hasn't turned up here or at work. I think he doesn't want to interfere with my earning capability in case he should need it. I looked in the yellow pages and there was an ad for flat fee uncontested divorce for £500 but I didn't have the money and I hated the idea of all the bother. I'll take care of it sometime. Maybe I'll get lucky and Troy will get run over by a bus or something.

In the meantime all I wanted was to pull myself together and not do anything foolish for a while. Right, so I had to go to that tango class. It didn't seem a bad idea at the time but now I'm entangled with this five-foot-seven-inch Phil. At least I can't marry him but that still leaves a lot of margin for error.

He wanted to see me again this week but I said I needed a little time to think about things. So he sent me my horoscope. Astrology, that's all I need. Another thing to worry about. This Catriona person says that Phil and I 'somehow mirror each other and mirror each other's capacity to mirror, and may both feel attracted and annoyed by qualities in the other you dislike in yourselves. You have both been badly treated – with violence or contempt – by your exes, and the suns of both of you are squared by Neptune.' Of course I'm the kind of person that, if I read about a disease, immediately I have all the symptoms. Suggestible is what I am. Very. I believed everything Catriona said and I sent my mind back to the Saturday of the tango class. Had I felt anything pulling me? Had I felt Neptune squaring my sun? I think maybe I did. 'Your Marses (libido, will power, assertiveness) are in square – a difficult challenging irritating aspect, and a strong trigger. Exciting but dangerous. Arousal and alertness.' There was more, but that was all I could take in just then. I wasn't understanding all of it, particularly that part about mirrors and the capacity to mirror. What is there in Phil that mirrors me? He said that his wife left him because he was a failure. I guess he feels like a failure. I certainly do. Whatever I've done has turned to shit. Except the artificial eyes. I don't seem to be doing any harm there.

I tried to understand what it is that's between Phil and me. If anything. No, I can feel *something*. Mirrors. Planets. Are we like two planets circling each other? No, one would be in orbit around the other. The smaller one. Is Phil in orbit around me? Neptune squaring my sun. At work I googled for Neptune. There were pictures of it, all blue and cold and far-away-looking. It used to have a Great Dark Spot but in 1994 it wasn't there any more. Phil and I both have dark spots.

He rang me up on the Thursday after we met at the tango class. 'Hi Barbara,' he said.

I liked how that sounded. 'Hi Phil.'

'Are we going to the tango class this Saturday?' he said.

'I'm thinking about it. Have you got a VCR?'

'Wouldn't be without one. Why?'

'If I rent a copy of *The Rainmaker* from Blockbuster, can we watch it at your place?'

'You don't have to rent one – I've got it. When do you want to come over?'

'Half hour?'

'Great. I'll meet you at Domino's Pizza so you don't get lost.'

All the way there I was thinking, Do we kiss? We did. Walking along the path beside the Underground lines we held hands. OK, I thought. Why not?

Phil's place was about what I expected. Lots of books, stacks of videos. A TV and a VCR. Desk and computer. Various boxes not yet unpacked. On the wall a large print of William Holman Hunt's *The Lady of Shalott*. Brian had used that picture in his lecture on the Pre-Raphaelites. ' "Out flew the web and floated wide," ' I quoted. ' "The mirror crack'd from side to side; / 'The curse is come upon me,' cried / The Lady of Shalott." '

'The poem doesn't say what the curse is,' said Phil. 'Only that she mustn't look down to Camelot. Maybe she needn't have laid herself down in that boat and died.'

'Did you put that picture up since meeting me?' I said.

'No, it's been up since I moved in eight months ago. Why do you ask?'

'Mirrors. Why did you choose that picture?'

'I don't know – it just spoke to me. She's "half-sick of shadows" and she's tangled in her own web. In the cracked mirror is the bright view of all that she can't have. Her feet are naked, she's never walked out into the world.'

'Are you sick of shadows and tangled in your own web with a mirror view of what you can't have?'

'Of course. Aren't you?'

'No, I'm down there in that river in a boat without a paddle. Not dead but drifting. Shall we order a pizza and watch the film?'

'OK, Barb,' said Phil. 'That'll be cosy.'

So we did that, and watching the film with beer and pizza was the cosiest thing I'd had in a long time. Kelly, the beaten wife, was *so* sweet, how could young lawyer Rudy not fall in love with her and want to protect her? I was with them all the way and I was actually shaking with the suspense of waiting for the scene where they finish off that bastard of a husband. Phil was holding me close to him and I knew he was being Rudy in his mind while I was being Kelly.

When it finally happened it was almost too much for me, I could hardly breathe. And when Kelly said to Rudy, 'Stop, give me the bat and leave. You were not here tonight!' I came close to spilling my beer. When it was over we hugged and kissed and didn't say anything for a while. Then we looked at each other and I said, 'Can I stay here tonight?'

'Barbara,' he said. 'I hope you stay with me for all the nights there are.'

I put my hand on his mouth. 'Don't say that. Nobody has all the nights there are.'

He kissed my hand and we went to bed.

3

PHIL OCKERMAN

The next morning when I heard Bertha/Barbara in the shower I felt as if the world was mine. The domesticity of getting ready for the day as a couple was balm to my soul. At breakfast we didn't say much but we smiled a lot. When Bertha/Barbara left to go to work she kissed me and said, 'Always call me Barbara. Have a terrific day.'

I kept on smiling after she left. I didn't want to make the bed, didn't want to lose the impression and the smell of her on the sheet and pillow and duvet. I'd have liked to think we really *were* a couple now but I knew that nothing was that simple or straightforward with Barbara. I played back the evening mentally, saw again the way she'd looked at me when she said, 'Can I stay here tonight?' Was it the film that had made it happen, the lovers finishing off the violent husband? Unworthy thought? Still—

Would she spend the night with me again? Not right away, I thought. I knew that she wouldn't like to be constantly pursued, would need some space. I wanted to send her some kind of a minimal next-morning message so I went to HMV looking for Gustav Holst's *The Planets*. I found that on a CD with Elgar's *Enigma Variations*, both conducted by Adrian Boult. *Enigma Variations* was first on the disc, so one had to get through the enigma to reach the planets. Reasonable, I thought. I wrote *X, Phil*, on a Post-it, put the CD in an envelope, and stuck it through her letterbox.

She rang me up that evening. 'Neptune, the Mystic, is my favourite,' she said. 'It *does* sound mystical, as if anything might happen, might be possible. It's open near and it's open far. I love it.'

'I thought you might. Did you listen to the Elgar?'

'Yes indeed – I had to go through the enigma to get to the planets. Here and there it sounded quite Neptuney.'

'I did a Google search,' I said, 'and this is a quote from Elgar: "The enigma I will not explain – its 'dark saying' must be left unguessed, and I warn you that the apparent connection between the Variations and the Theme is often of the slightest texture; further, through and over the whole set another and larger theme 'goes', but is not played . . ." Barbara.'

'What?'

'I just wanted to say your name.'

' "Another and larger theme goes but is not played." The larger theme can't really be played, can it? There aren't the notes for it . . . But it's the one that matters. Phil?'

'What?'

'Just wanted to say your name. Phil, are you afraid?'

'Yes.'

'Of what?'

'Everything.'

'Me too.'

'Want to be afraid together with Chinese takeaway and a film?'

'OK. I'll bring the wine. What do you think, red or white?'

'You decide. Any film preferences?'

'You decide. See you in a little, Phil.'

'Till soon, Barb.' I looked at my DVDs and videos. Thriller, feelgood, western, comedy, romance, what? I decided on *The Cooler*, with William H. Macy, Maria Bello, and Alec Baldwin. It's got winning and losing, bad luck, good luck, love and a great ending. I'd already watched it twice.

I rang up Mayflower and ordered won ton soup, spring rolls, sweet and sour pork, special foo yung, and egg fried rice for two, then I closed my eyes, imagining Barbara coming down the North End Road. I saw her smiling face, saw her breath in the air, heard her footsteps against the background noise. The colours of the lights in the crisp dark of the evening, almost I could taste them. Now she'll be at Ryman, I thought. Now at Waitrose. Now she's in the Fulham Road. Now at Domino's Pizza, no – she won't be there yet because she's probably getting the wine at Waitrose. But then I didn't see anything but darkness and I had that dropping sensation you get sometimes when falling asleep. 'What?' I said.

I wanted to go out to meet her but the Mayflower delivery was on the way so I waited until it arrived, then I went out to the path along Eel Brook Common and she ran into my arms all breathless and shaking. 'What is it?' I said. 'What happened?'

'Troy,' she said. 'I went to Oddbins in Harwood Road, I thought he'd have been at work already but he was just passing as I came out. "Going to a party?" he said. He pulled me around the corner into Effie Road, past El Metro and into the common. Then, with no one to see him do it, he grabbed me by the hair but before he could swing me around I hit him with the Minervois. Knocked him out but I broke the bottle.'

'Where is he now?'

'Probably still flat on his face on the path.'

'Is he badly hurt? Should we call an ambulance?'

'I don't see why. That's an occupational hazard in his line of work — he'll come round by himself or somebody will give him first or second aid, whatever.'

Now I began to see her in a new light as someone to whom violence came easily. If she'd hit Troy hard enough with that bottle to knock him out he might even be dead or at least concussed. In the movies people get sapped with gun butts and all kinds of hard objects and it does them no permanent harm but real life isn't like that.

'The way you're looking at me you must've led a very sheltered life,' she said, 'and in the meantime the wine's gone and the Chinese takeaway'll be getting cold.'

'Sorry, Barbara. I've got a bottle of red at home and the food's only just been delivered – it'll be all right. But are *you* all right?' I'd have thought she'd be trembling after an encounter like that but she seemed perfectly calm.

'I'm OK,' she said. 'I'll be fine when we settle down with food and drink and a video at your place.'

'I've got a great movie for you, *The Cooler*.'

'What's it about?'

'Winning and losing, good luck and bad luck. Love. Mainly it's a love story.'

'Could we watch *The Rainmaker* again?'

'Sure, Barb, anything you like.' Jesus, I thought, that film really is a turn-on for her.

The food was still warm and the wine was so good that we finished it too quickly and carried on with beer. Barbara was squeezing my arm so hard she left bruises. 'Let's get on with it,' she said to the screen when the legal action and courtroom scenes went on too long. 'Bastard!' she said when the husband yelled at Kelly and threw a bowlful of soup on her in the hospital. 'You'll get yours, you bloody wife-beater! Just wait!' When Rudy and Kelly beat him to death she said, 'Yes!' and smothered me with kisses. 'You ever wish you were six inches taller, Phil?'

'Most of the time. Do *you* wish I were six inches taller?'

'Actually, it's not the *size* that matters, it's what you *do* with it.'

'What are we talking about, Babs?'

'You, Phil, the total five foot seven of you.'

'You're going to make me very uncomfortable if you keep harping on about my shortness, Babsy.'

A very serious kiss this time. 'But I can make you very comfortable too, can't I?'

'We'll see about that,' I said. 'Are we going to the tango class tomorrow? Or is this tomorrow?'

'The room's going round,' she said. 'I'll think about it after I throw up.'

'This way, please,' I said, and led her to the bathroom.

When Barbara had finished being sick she said, 'Would you get my bag for me, please?' When I gave it to her she took out a toothbrush. I tried to act unsurprised. When she'd cleaned her teeth and washed her face she said, 'Give me a shirt.'

'A shirt?'

'In the movies the woman wakes up wearing a man's shirt, so give me one and put me to bed.'

'My pleasure,' I said. I tucked her in and kissed her goodnight.

'Aren't you coming to bed?' she said.

'Not yet. I want to sit at my desk for a while and think about you in my shirt in my bed.'

'You like to think about me?'

'Yes.'

'That's nice. I'll think about you too.' She fell asleep immediately. I went into the living room and walked around hugging myself for a while, then I went to my desk. I sat there thinking about Barbara, then I went to my computer and watched the cursor on the word processor flickering like a snake's tongue. Mimi had said that *Hope of a Tree* was 'a put-together thing trying to pass itself off as a novel', and she was right. It was about a painter whose wife had committed suicide. For a long time after her death he couldn't work but then he met a new woman etc. Why hadn't I done better? And why did that come to mind now? I reached for the Bible in the stack by the desk and turned to Job 14:7-9:

> For there is hope of a tree, if it be cut down,
> that it will sprout again, and that the tender
> branch thereof will not cease.
> 8 Though the root thereof wax old in the earth,
> and the stock thereof die in the ground;
> 9 Yet through the scent of water it will bud,
> and bring forth boughs like a plant.

I put a blank page up on the screen and thought about a title for what might or might not be my next novel. I closed my eyes and saw Barbara asleep in my bed. I opened my eyes and typed *The Scent of Water*. OK, the scent of water. What about it? I had determined not to use the current events of my life, I wanted to keep Barbara private and separate. So what was *The Scent of Water* going to be about? No idea. 'Never mind,' I said to myself. 'You've got a title and that's a start.' Then I got ready for bed and climbed in beside Barbara. She was snoring so loudly that she sounded like a 747 passing very low over the house.

Between her snoring and the deliciousness of her solid warmth I was a long time falling asleep. I lay awake thinking about Troy Wallis and his violence to Barbara. Although actually he might now qualify as a battered husband. Indeed, he might be lying dead on the path by the common. I'd never seen him and the only visible evidence of his violence was the bruising on Barbara's arms. Did he exist? Here I was falling in love with this woman and I wasn't even sure whether or not she was lying to me.

Nothing but sleep happened that night, and when Barbara got up in the morning she groaned. All she had for breakfast was coffee, then she kissed me, said, 'See you,' and left.

'When?' I called after her.

'Don't know,' with a shrug.

I went to my desk and accosted the word machine. It looked at me as if I were a stranger. 'Don't give me that,' I said. 'Without me you're nothing.'

Big talk, it snapped back. What have you done for me lately?

I checked my e-mail for the second time, looked in on Ellen MacArthur's website to see how she was doing in her solo circumnavigation of the globe, and worried with her about the high pressure area ahead. Then I suddenly couldn't remember where my copy of *the lives and times of archy & mehitabel* was. Looked for it but no luck, so rather than lose the whole day in a fruitless search I ordered a used copy (the book was out of print) from AbeBooks. By then it was nearly lunchtime so I thought I might as well get some air.

I went out to Eel Brook Common and walked along the path where Barbara had said she'd knocked Troy out with the Minervois. There was no broken glass. The cleaners had already been and would have swept it up. There were some dark stains on the paving that might have been wine or blood or both but I couldn't be sure. I was disgusted with myself for doubting Barbara but the uncertainty persisted. I recalled what I'd learned about the tango, how the partners have to trust each other, have to be completely tuned in to each other. I remembered our bodies touching all last night and her vulnerable nakedness in my shirt, remembered how it felt to hold her in that beginners' class: there wasn't trust but there was openness and a willingness to explore possibilities. If Barbara and I could become really good tango dancers, what might not develop? but I didn't want to be in a crowd of learners again. Maybe if we went for private tuition?

She didn't turn up that evening so I phoned her.

'Barbara,' I said, 'it's me.'

'Hi,' she said. 'I was just about to go out.'

'Oh.' Go out where? With whom? Mustn't ask. 'I thought we might try some private tango tuition.'

'What for?'

'So we could concentrate on getting beyond the beginners' stage.'

'Why?' She didn't sound like the woman who'd slept next to me last night.

'I think it would feel good to tango well, don't you?'

'What does it cost?' As if she'd never smothered me with kisses and thrown up in my bathroom.

'Forty pounds an hour.'

'I can't spend twenty pounds on a tango lesson.'

'No, no, this is my treat.'

'I don't want you to spend forty pounds on a lesson for us either.' Her voice was tapping its foot, eager to put down the phone.

'Why not?' I said. 'It's no big deal, it's less than dinner for two at any decent restaurant.'

'It's not the same thing and you know it. Listen, I have to go.'

I could hear in her voice that I wasn't going to see her for a while. Was mine the sensitivity of a natural loser? I had an upcoming workshop to do at Morley College so I moved my mind to that and made my Barbara thoughts wait until I could give them my full attention. Of course they kept hammering on the door but I told myself I'd have to get used to that.

4

BERTHA STRUNK

I wasn't surprised when Brian Adderley turned up at the Lichtheim studio for a check-up; that was a regular thing with their clients. Sometimes I used to wonder what I'd say when I saw him again. The time we'd spent together wasn't the kind of thing you forget, and lying in bed beside Troy I'd find myself remembering nights with Brian.

So there he was. He looked very well and very prosperous. Not that he was fashionably dressed – he was as scruffy as ever – but he looked as if he could buy anything without asking the price first. 'You look to be in good shape,' he said, and kissed me on the cheeks.

'So do you,' I said, and after Karl did the check-up Brian and I went to The Blue Posts and sank a couple of pints. 'I still owe you some Dubai money,' he said.

'No, you don't. I didn't mind posing for the paintings but I really couldn't square it with Artemisia if I took money for it.'

'You've got fancy scruples,' he said.

'Everybody draws the line somewhere, I think.'

'Even I. Would you believe that since you left I haven't been with any other woman?'

'No, I wouldn't.'

'All right, I didn't actually go cold turkey but it was like being alone. Can you believe that?'

'Almost. At least it's a nice compliment.'

'So are you with anyone now?'

'I'm married but I'm not with my husband any more.'

'Why not?'

'One beating was enough.'

'How could you marry a man stupid enough to beat you?'

'I'm not very clever myself. You may have noticed.'

'You've got someone else?'

'Sort of. It's too soon to say.'

'Who is he?'

'No one you know. He's a writer.'

'What's his name?'

'Phil Ockerman.'

'The guy who wrote *Hope of a Tree*?'

'Have you read it?'

'Yes, and it was real crap. He uses words well enough but it was really just a put-together thing trying to pass for a novel. Have *you* read it?'

'No. How are things between you and your wife?'

'We're divorced. She's got the house and the kids and

a lot of money and I've moved here. I've got a house in Cheyne Walk.'

'You must have struck it rich.'

'Von Augenblick doesn't only have contacts in Dubai, he's got the whole Middle East pretty well covered, and Judith & Co. go down a bomb with his clientele.'

We were quiet for a while, then a white-haired woman nearby leaned our way and said, 'Actually, *Hope of a Tree* had quite a few good things in it. You can't expect strong plots from Ockerman, his novels are mainly character-driven.' Her face might not have been beautiful when she was young but looked very classy now and there was something in her voice – it was low and husky – that made me think she must have had an exciting past and a lot of lovers. I'd noticed her when she came in; she was taller than I and had a long slim black velvet bag slung from her shoulder. It knocked against the table when she sat down and it didn't sound like an umbrella. She saw me looking at it and slid it partly out of the bag. It was a baseball bat. I thought of *The Rainmaker* and I couldn't help smiling. Sometimes it's nothing but baseball bats. A sign?

'A Louisville Slugger,' she said. 'His name is Irv.'

' "His", not "Its",' said Brian. 'Has that bat got a history?'

'It has,' she said. 'But you wouldn't believe it. I wouldn't have believed it myself if I didn't know that form and emptiness are the same.'

'Not a lot of people know that,' Brian said. 'What're you drinking? You need a refill.'

'Directors,' she said. 'But just a half please. Vodka used to be my tipple but the ravages of time forced me to switch to beer, and even that puts me to sleep if I'm not careful.'

Brian went to the bar and got refills for all of us, then he said to the woman with the baseball bat, 'Tell us the story, please. I'm Brian Adderley. This is Bertha Strunk.'

'Hi,' she said. 'My name is Grace Kowalski. The bat is named after a friend who's no longer with us. Some years back he and I and a few others were involved in some very strange goings-on. Do you believe in ghosts?'

'Yes,' said Brian.

'Sometimes,' I said.

'I hang out with more ghosts than I do with live people,' said Grace.

'That's part of getting old, I guess,' said Brian.

'It sure is,' said Grace. 'Do you believe in vampires?'

'Metaphorically or literally?' said Brian.

'The kind that actually suck blood,' said Grace.

'Not yet,' said Brian.

'Likewise,' I said.

'Just asking,' said Grace.

'Do you?' I said.

'Takes all kinds,' said Grace. 'What do you do?' she asked me.

'I paint eyeballs for artificial eyes,' I said.

68

'And you?' she said to Brian.

'I'm a painter,' he said. 'Pictures on canvas. Are you retired?'

'Not yet,' said Grace. 'I make jewellery and I sell it in my shop, All That Glisters, just up the street.'

I said, 'I pass it every day on my way to work.'

'Small world,' said Grace. 'No unknown places any more. Except perhaps in people.'

'I'd like to do a portrait of you,' said Brian. 'Will you pose for me?'

'I thought you'd never ask,' said Grace. 'But I don't do nudity unless it's essential to the plot.'

'Sometimes a plot can take you unawares,' said Brian, and raised his glass to her. He'll flirt with whatever female comes into his field of vision. He and Grace exchanged phone numbers and Brian and I said goodbye and got up to leave.

'See you,' said Grace. 'Have a good whatever.'

It was twilight when we came out into Berwick Street. 'Where to?' said Brian.

'Cheyne Walk?' I said.

'Bertha, you read my mind,' he said. He hailed a cab and off we went. Hearing him call me Bertha made me think of Phil with a little twinge of guilt. Not a big twinge, just a little one. Phil and I still didn't really know where we were with each other, but with Brian I knew exactly where we were and I was comfortable with it. No commitment, no problems, just a good time in bed in a beautiful house. Was I being amoral? Well, you know what they say: there are parts of the human body that have no conscience.

But the part of my body that *has* got a conscience is my brain. And lying there beside Brian I was feeling guilty about what I'd done and hadn't done with my life so far. Here I was, thirty-seven years old and painting artificial eyes. Back when Brian was my teacher he'd told me to loosen up and I'd done that, but not on canvas. Then my attempts to develop as an artist had gradually faded away while my talents as a mistress improved all the time. Was it too late to find out if I could be any kind of a painter other than an eyeball one? On the other hand, if I'd had any real talent I'd have done something with it by now. It's not just a matter of talent – you've got to have the drive and the character to do something with it, whether it's painting, snooker, or tennis. Brian was asleep and snoring. 'Cheryl,' he mumbled. That wasn't his wife's name.

After a while I fell asleep and dreamt that Grace Kowalski offered to lend me her bat. 'He ain't heavy,' she said. 'He's my Irving.' But it *was* heavy, I could hardly lift it. I woke up and the room wasn't as dark as it had been. There were framed sketches on the wall. Me, nude. No clothes but I hadn't felt as naked when I posed as I did now.

5

PHIL OCKERMAN

She was with another man; that was a certainty. It was as if I could feel his weight on her as he enjoyed what was now denied to me. I ground my teeth and tried to move my mind elsewhere. Without much success.

I could see a space without Barbara stretching out in front of me for miles and miles: a desert. And I was two vast and trunkless legs of stone standing in the middle of it with my shattered visage, half-sunk, lying nearby. Well, that's how it is sometimes: boundless and bare, the lone and level sands stretch far away. Deal with it.

Ordinarily I get through each day by finding things to look forward to, like a mountain climber moving from one handhold to the next: breakfast; *The Times*; the post; scanning the TV schedule and setting the timer to record films that look promising; sending and answering e-mails; lunch and the first beer of the day; a few pages of Elizabeth Gaskell with my sandwich; then a nap. In between I put in some time staring at *The Scent of Water*, my lonesome title with no first line under it. That part of the day I haven't really been looking forward to, and I do it again in the evening. And there are the classes I teach at Morley and the private workshops that use up three afternoons and two evenings every week.

If I could follow the advice I give my students I might possibly achieve even a whole first paragraph. I draw on haiku heavily for this. A common complaint is, 'When I have a blank sheet of paper in front of me I feel lost.' For this I have committed to memory lines by Ryusui:

Mayoigo no
naku naku tsukamu
hotaru kana

The lost child,
crying, crying, but still
catching the fireflies.

A blank sheet of paper is a very dark night in which we lost children can't help crying, I tell them. The thing is to keep catching fireflies. I constantly remind myself of that but this seems not to be a firefly season.

I listened to the first track of the *Enigma Variations*; the theme came out of a distant silence, veiled and mysterious, then it grew and unfolded, always in the light and shadow of the larger unplayed theme. OK, I have no right to expect anything but the unfolding. Maybe there's nothing in it for me. That's life, yes?

I cursed myself for being so dependent on Barbara. Lots of men get through life without a woman; why couldn't I? Also, this might not be a permanent condition – she might be back. But I didn't like being kept dangling like this. It was cold, it was grey, it was raining. Good. I went to the National Gallery. I stood on the porch for a few minutes looking down on Trafalgar Square. Spray from the fountains drifting in the rain. Red sightseeing buses. Nelson on his column, secure in his place above it all. That's the way to do it, I thought, and went inside.

I'm a heavy user of the National Gallery. Depending on what condition my condition is in I usually know what I need for my fix. Sometimes it's Claude, other times de Hooch or maybe van Hoogstraten's peepshow or the van de Veldes marine paintings. But today I didn't know what would do it for me.

I was drifting from one room to another when I paused in Room 41 at the Daumier that shows Don Quixote on Rosinante charging a flock of sheep while Sancho on Dapple quenches his thirst from a gourd. Daumier didn't do any large paintings – they're all medium-sized to small. This one was 40 × 64 centimetres and it was a sketch, not a finished picture. But the thing about Daumier is that all of his pictures, regardless of size, are *big*. And his sketches are usually the biggest of all because they're the freeest and the quickly done chiaroscuro is nothing short of metaphysical.

I was thinking about Don Quixote and Sancho when a tall young woman took up a position a foot or two away. Her close attention to the Daumier already marked her as someone to be reckoned with and her looks did nothing to dispel that impression. She stood there shaking her head a little and moving her lips, then she took a pad of music paper from her rucksack, sat down on the floor, and began to fill the staves with notes and words.

'Does this happen often with you?' I said.

She held up a finger to pause me while she finished a bar. 'All the time,' she said.

'Not only with Don Quixote or Daumier, then?'

'I like Cervantes and Daumier both – this painting is what got me going just now but it's not specifically a Don Quixote song.' A slight South African accent.

'Can you say what it's about?'

'Yes, it's about being true to your craziness.'

'Will you have a coffee with me when you're ready to stand up?'

She got up from her cross-legged position without using her hands. 'I'm ready now, but it'll have to be a fast coffee because I'm due in Soho in three quarters of an hour.'

'The cafeteria won't be crowded now, so we can get one there quickly. Are you here for a visit?' I said as we walked towards the Sainsbury Wing.

'Three weeks,' she said, 'mostly talking to record company execs. Then I go back to Cape Town.'

'Have you got a contract?'

'My agent's working on it. Are you American?'

'Yes, but I've been living here for the last twelve years.' By this time we were sitting at a table having our coffee and I was able to study her closely. Brown hair which she wore long and straight; blue eyes; large nose; wide mouth; high forehead. Not exactly a beauty but the overall effect was impressive. She reminded me of champion athletes I'd seen on TV. She had the look of a winner and that made her face add up to more than the sum of its parts.

'What are you?' she said. 'A hypnotist?'

'Please forgive my staring. I'm a writer. What's your name?'

'Constanze Webber. What's yours?'

'Phil Ockerman. I doubt that you've heard of me.'

'Oh, but I have. I was watching *The Culture Show* the other night and Germaine Greer said that *Hope of a Tree* was a shallow male fantasy that didn't add up to a novel.'

'An opinion shared by one or two others,' I said.

'Still, the title from Job intrigued me. Does your man feel like a tree that's been cut down?'

'Are you an Old Testament user?'

'Now and then. Job is one of my favourite books. He bears his afflictions with style. *Does* your man feel like a tree that's been cut down?'

'Yes, he does.'

'There's a copy of *Hope of a Tree* at the house where I'm staying. I'll read it and I'll probably like it.'

'And you so young and apparently unafflicted. How old are you – twenty-four, twenty-five?'

'Twenty-five. There are all kinds of afflictions, Phil. They don't always show. How old are you?'

'I'm forty.'

'Forty seems very far away from where I am now. I can't imagine where I'll be at that age.'

'The years have a way of sneaking up on you,' I said. She looked at her watch. 'I must go.'

'Can I see you again?' I said.

'All right – I'll be with friends in Wimbledon for the rest of this week; you can phone me there.' She wrote the number on a napkin. 'Then I'm going back to Cape Town for a couple of weeks. Don't get up, stay and finish your coffee. See you.' And off she went. I'd have liked to walk her to Soho, all five foot ten of her, but she'd clearly told me not to so I finished my coffee and had another, this time with a cheese Danish.

When I got home there was a card saying that Royal Mail had tried to deliver a parcel. I went round to the sorting office to pick it up: a bat-shaped box from Louisville, Kentucky. I carried it back to the house as if it were a loaded gun. I took it out of the box and there it was, my GENUINE *Barbara Strozzi* LOUISVILLE SLUGGER. Blonde wood. Ash? Thirty-four inches long. I weighed it on the kitchen scale: one kilo. Long, heavy, dangerous. I got a good grip on it, took up my stance, looked towards the mound, knocked the dirt off my spikes. Pitcher looks in for the sign, nods, goes into his windup, and here comes Troy Wallis, right over the plate. No, no – only kidding. I leaned the Louisville Slugger in a corner and sat down at the word machine and thought about Job for a while, how one day Satan showed up with the sons of God and when the Lord asked him where he was coming from he said, 'From going to and fro in the earth, and from walking up and down in it.' That's the heart of the matter right there – he's always around ready to lead the unwary into mischief with the first available Constanze or whatever else offers. And of course idle hands are the Devil's workshop, everybody knows that. 'So let's get cracking, Phil,' I said. 'OK,' I answered, 'just warming up in the bullpen.' I put the *Enigma Variations* in the player, picked up the phone, ordered a pizza from Domino's, opened a bottle of The Wine Society's French Full Red and poured myself a glass. Put *The Rainmaker* in the video, and when the pizza arrived I ate it, drank about two thirds of the red, fell asleep in my chair halfway through the film, and dreamed that Constanze Webber was walking far ahead of me through a dim and narrow space. 'Wait!' I shouted, 'I can explain!' She looked back once, then turned and walked on. I woke up and dialled Barbara's number. 'Barbara?' I said when the phone was picked up at the other end.

'You have a wrong number,' said a tight voice.

'I meant to say Bertha,' I said. 'You must be Hilary.'

'And who are you?'

'Phil Ockerman, I'm a friend of Bertha's.'

'Odd that you couldn't remember her name.'

'Anyhow, is she available?'

'No, she isn't. Goodbye.'

'Thanks so much,' I said to the silence.

I was sitting in my TV chair then with my hand on the round part at the end of the bat handle. I moved the handle around as if it were the control stick of an aeroplane. Then I wrote down the telephone number of Jimmy Maloney's, put on a jacket and went out to the Fulham Road.

I stationed myself near the bus stop diagonally opposite the club and looked at the big man standing in the doorway. Dark suit, dark polo neck. Did he have a plaster on his head? Couldn't see one. Took my mobile out of my pocket and dialled the number. 'Jimmy Maloney's,' said a growly voice over a lot of background noise.

'Is Troy Wallis on the door tonight?' I said.

'Who's this?'

'Nobody he knows. Somebody gave me a message to give him. Is he there?'

The bartender or whoever it was hung up. I kept my eyes on the door and saw a man who looked like a bartender come to where the bouncer was and talk briefly with him. So that was Troy Wallis. About six four, fourteen or fifteen stone. Right, thanks very much.

I'd read in the paper that Mercury would be low in the west and Venus out of sight. Not too comfortable with that. The moon was in its first quarter, the vernal equinox only three days away. I looked up at the sky and made out Ursa Major and Ursa Minor, Polaris, Cassiopeia, and Draco. Draco looked aggressive. I was too ignorant to identify the other constellations. I felt uneasy with the forces affecting me and longed for some guidance from Catriona.

I thought of the Louisville Slugger leaning in its corner, saw the name *Barbara Strozzi* engraved on it. I hadn't listened to her music for what seemed a long time and now I hungered for it. I walked home through the Friday-night noise in the Fulham Road, then through the quiet of the path between the common and the District Line. An Upminster train rumbled and clattered past, people printed on the windows as on a tin toy. Crowded but lonely, that train. Maybe all the passengers were headed for a pleasant evening or even a good time; but the train was a lonely tin toy.

At home I put on the *Arie, Cantate & Lamenti* disc. The voice of Mona Spagele came out of the silence with 'L'Eraclito Amoroso'. Up and up it circled, obedient to Venus and the moon, to the planetary spring tides and neap tides of love and the death of love. The song was a lament but the beauty of it was Strozzi's thank-offering for being alive. One doesn't beg for constant guidance, I thought; one gives oneself and takes what comes.

Well, yes. That had a good sound to it but what did it mean exactly? Getting up from my chair to pour myself a drink I knocked the top book off the nearest stack: *Walt Whitman: The Complete Poems*. As it hit the floor it fell open to pages 462 and 463. I picked it up and read:

A Noiseless, Patient Spider

A noiseless, patient spider,
I mark'd where on a little promontory it stood
   isolated,
Mark'd how to explore the vacant vast surrounding,
It launch'd forth filament, filament, filament, out
   of itself,
Ever unreeling them, ever tirelessly speeding them.

And you, O my soul where you stand,
In measureless oceans of space,
Ceaselessly musing, venturing, throwing, seeking the
   spheres to connect them,
Till the bridge you need will be form'd, till the
   ductile anchor hold,
Till the gossamer thread you fling catch somewhere,
   O my Soul.

'You're the man, Walt,' I said, and as a change from Glenfiddich pour'd myself a large Laphroaig. While getting myself around the smoky peat-bog flavour I considered where next to fling my gossamer. Constanze had written a song about being true to your craziness. OK, I thought, and rang the Wimbledon number. A young South African male answered.

'Hello,' I said, 'this is Phil Ockerman. Is Constanze available?'

'Hang on,' he said, and put the phone down to shout, ' 'Stanze! It's for you.'

Constanze appeared presently. 'Hello,' she said. 'Who's this?'

'Phil Ockerman.'

'Oh, *Hope of a Tree*.'

'Actually, it's hope of seeing you before you leave for Cape Town. Is that possible?'

'I'm kind of pressed for time. What did you want to see me about?'

'I wanted to hear more about your music.'

'Oh. What for?'

'I'm a writer – I get interested in all kinds of things.'

'Ah, professional interest.'

'That, but mainly I just want to see more of you – I'm being true to my craziness.'

'That's all very well, Phil, but it takes two to tango.'

'It also takes two to have a conversation and a coffee but never mind. I'll see you around. Or not.' I rang off.

'I'm embarrassed for you,' I said to myself.

'Twenty-five-year olds!' I replied. 'What do you expect?'

The phone rang. 'Hello,' I said.

'It's me, Constanze. I don't have to be anywhere tomorrow until late afternoon. Can you meet me at Putney Bridge tube station at eleven?'

'OK.'

'See you then.'

I listened to Barbara Strozzi for a while before going to sleep and dreaming of a foreign city with very wide streets and cold northern sunlight.

The next morning was sunny and mild. Constanze was right on time. 'I've brought some music with me,' she said. 'Let's sit by the river while you listen.' We went into Bishop's Park, and from a bench near the bridge watched an eight stroking past towards Barnes, bright droplets falling from the oars on each return and the coxswain's voice coming to us small and urgent over the water.

Constanze handed me her little CD player and headphones. 'Here's a working recording of one of my songs called "Blue Mountains".'

I started the disc. Over the sound of instruments tuning up Constanze's voice said, ' "Used-To-Be" take three.' After a short silence there was the wavering melody of a flute, then a violin and a cello came in over a quietly pulsing drumbeat. I imagined a distant escarpment under a wide sky. The flute faded out and the strings and drums continued under a woman's voice speaking low and breathily, as in the intimacy of the small hours. A naked voice making itself heard in the darkness. At first I thought it was a black woman, then I recognised the voice as Constanze's:

Kopelo, kopelo e e iketlileng mo tsebeng ya moja
Ee, kopelo ee ritibetseng e le runi
Jaaka phala ya selemo se se fetileny mo tsebeng yame
Sona Sepoko, ke go raa ke go raa
Ke tlaabo ke aka go rileng?
Sone Sepoko sa maloba-le-maabane Aiyeeah!

Understanding not a word, I was filled with a great sadness. 'What language is that?' I asked.

'Setswana,' she said. Her voice on the disc paused. The music came up and she sang with it wordlessly and very low. Then she continued speaking:

Aiyeeah! Kutlobotlhoko ya sona ta se opela
Sona Sepoko sa maloba-le-maabane! Se a opela,
Se a opela sona sa fa loapi le ne le tlhapile,
dithaba di boitshega letsatsi ke bosigo jwa lona
di ya lolololo dinoka di elela!

The music changed, the drums became more urgent. Constanze's voice went higher and the words came more quickly:

Utlwa fa ke go rao Nao, O itse tsa moloba-le-maabane
Kwa re tswang gona mmogo, fa lorato le ne re aparetse
le tletse mo pelong tsa rona, aiyeeah!
Le kae jaanong, le sietse kae?
Gore loapi le be le thibile jaona, dithaba di sa
ntsikinye, dinoka di kgadile jaana! Aiyeeah ka

iketlo mo tsebeng ya moja kopelo ya sepoko sa
moloba-le-maabane. Mo tsebeng ya molema go utlwala
fela kgakalo ya dikgang tsa seseng, pherethlano
mo mebileng le modumo wa tse di fetileng.

Always the sadness came to me in those words I
couldn't understand. The vowels and the consonants
had a life of their own that seemed also to be my
life. I remembered how it was when Mimi and I
were first in love, the newness of the world. And I
remembered the sadness when love had gone and
we stood in a dry riverbed. The flute was alone
again and I could see for miles. High overhead a
hawk circled, sharp against the blue. The violin and
cello and drums came in and over them Constanze
singing in English:

> Singing, singing tiny in my right ear,
> in my right ear only, yes! Singing tiny
> like the summer's last cicada in my ear,
> a ghost! That's what I'm telling you –
> why should I lie? The ghost of used-to-be!
> Aiyeeah!

Her voice was thrilling, with a wildness under the words
that sometimes almost whispered, sometimes soared.
The sound of the instruments and her voice together
seemed layered with before and after:

> The sadness of it singing there, that
> ghost of used-to-be! It sings, it sings of
> when the sky was very wide, the mountains
> were magic, a day and a night were for ever
> and the rivers never dried up.

Hearing the English now with the Setswana behind it I smelled the sun-warm grass, tasted used-to-be on my tongue.

Now Constanze's was more urgent as the words came faster:

> Hear what I'm saying! You know that used-to-be,
> you know we lived there, you and I, when love
> was with us, when love was in our hearts, aiyeeah!

> Where is it now, where has it gone, that the sky
> has become little, the mountains nothing special,
> the rivers all dry? Aiyeeah!

> Tiny in my right ear sings that ghost of
> used-to-be. Loud in my left ear is the news on the
> hour, the traffic in the streets, the roar of
> all-gone.

Silence and the sound of traffic on Putney Bridge. I opened my eyes. There was the river and I was in London again. 'You look sad,' said Constanze.

' "Used-To-Be" is a sad song,' I said.

'Oh shit,' she said. 'That was meant to be "Blue Mountains" in the player. I didn't mean for you to hear "Used-To-Be."'

'Why not?'

'I'm still working on it.'

'Is there a ghost in your ear, Constanze?'

'Always. Africa is full of ghosts.'

'So is every place. I was wondering if the song is about a particular used-to-be in your life.'

'Can we talk about something else?'

'Sorry for the intrusion. It's a beautiful song and a terrific performance. Is anyone else doing anything like this?'

'Not that I know of.'

'How did you become so fluent in Setswana?'

'I learned it from my nanny. She was from Bophu-tatswana and her name was Omphile which means God's gift. When I was a baby she carried me around on her back in a towel while she did the household chores. She had a baby of her own who was living with Omphile's mother in the homeland – that's what Bophutatswana was during apartheid.'

'So Omphile raised you while the grandmother raised her child.' I had to shake my head at that.

'That's how it was,' said Constanze. 'Nannies usually had to speak Afrikaans or English in the houses where they worked but my parents thought it was good for me to learn Omphile's language.'

'Why did you speak the song in Setswana?'

'I wrote it in that language and then translated it into English. I think my songs in Setswana, that's how they come to me. Setswana has Omphile in it and her people and where they came from. I like to keep this inside me, so let's not talk about it any more. I read *Hope of a Tree* last night.'

'And?'

'I like the way you write and I liked the ideas in the book but I didn't think it was a very good novel.'

'Can you say why?'

Constanze thought about it for a while. Her face was one that changed from moment to moment; now, when she was mentally rehearsing what she would say, she looked about eighteen. 'There wasn't really any hope in it,' she said. 'It just runs downhill in a straight line. It starts with Cynthia standing on Clifton Bridge looking down at the Avon Gorge. Is she going to jump? Sam thinks so. He says, "It's a long way down." She says, "It's a short trip though." He tries to distract her, says, "Have you seen the camera obscura at the observatory?" And of course she says, "I don't need to – I've been living in a dark chamber for a long time." So you wonder if Sam is a suicide saver, the way some people are drunk savers. It never works, and you know it won't work for Sam and Cynthia so it's no surprise when it doesn't.'

'Life is like that sometimes,' I said.

'Sure, but why bother with that kind of story?'

'I was trying to do a story where one thing follows

another in a chain of cause and effect that goes right down the line to its inevitable end. Have you seen Kaurismäki's film *The Match Factory Girl*?'

'No.'

'That's a straight cause-and-effect film. Iris, the match factory girl, after being treated badly by her mother, her mother's live-in boyfriend, and a man who picked her up in a bar, puts rat poison in their drinks and in the end is led off by the police. Very bleak, but it leaves you feeling good.'

'Ah, but there's a positive element in that. She fought back with the rat poison. Cynthia and Sam didn't do anything like that so there's nothing to feel good about.'

'You're right. I must do better. Fancy some lunch?'

She looked at her watch. 'I can't – I'm meeting my agent for lunch in Soho.'

'What's his name? Maybe I've heard of him.'

'I doubt it – he's from Jo'burg, an old friend of the family, Teddy von Augenblick.'

'*Theodor* von Augenblick?'

'That's him.'

'Actually I *have* heard of him. My ex-wife works at the Nikolai Chevorski Gallery and he was in there trying to promote some painter whose talent wasn't as big as his canvases. I haven't seen the paintings or met von Augenblick myself.'

'Teddy has his finger in all kinds of pies – I don't know anything about his painters.'

'But you trust him to represent you.'

'Why shouldn't I? I've known him since I was a little girl. As I've said, he's an old friend of the family and he's been like an uncle to me.'

'Uncle Teddy.'

'Yes, that's what I used to call him.'

'Did he use to take you on his lap?'

'That's what uncles do, isn't it? What're you getting at?'

'Nothing. Being a writer, I'm always interested in a character's back story.'

'I'd rather you backed away from mine, it's not that interesting.'

'If you say. Could I have the words to "Used-To-Be", both the Setswana and the English?'

'What for?'

'It's a lament and I'm into laments.'

'I'll send you the words after we do the final recording.'

'You don't trust me, do you?'

'Not really. I have to go now.'

'When can I see you again?'

'I'll call you after I get back from Cape Town.'

I walked her to Putney Bridge, and even for that short distance she stayed a little way ahead of me. At the entrance to the tube station she said, 'See you,' and was gone.

6

BARBARA STRUNK

I was sitting naked on Brian's unmade bed on a Saturday morning. Alone. I'd had a lie-in and Brian hadn't woken me. I didn't hear him anywhere, no sounds but the traffic on the Embankment. Naked me on the bed; naked me on the wall. I wasn't exactly thinking but I was *thinking* about thinking when I heard the front door open and close downstairs. Then there were quick footsteps on the stairs, a female voice said, 'Bri?' and a girl who couldn't have been more than twenty burst into the room. Blonde, good figure, very pretty – well, she would be, wouldn't she. And she had a key because she'd let herself in. 'Oh,' she said, 'are you posing for him?'

'Not at the moment,' I said. 'Are you Cheryl?'

'Yes. Has Brian mentioned me to you?'

'Briefly.'

'And you,' she said, 'you're . . .?'

'Just leaving,' I said. I went to the bathroom but didn't bother to take a shower. When I came out

Cheryl wasn't in the bedroom. I picked my clothes up off the floor, got dressed, walked up to the King's Road and caught an 11 bus.

When I got off in Harwood Road I was about halfway between my flat and Phil's place. Which way will my feet take me? I thought. I watched them take me back to Moore Park Road and over to Eel Brook Common. No, I thought, not with the smell of sex with Brian still on me. I turned back and went up Harwood to Fulham Broadway and home to Sir Cliff Richard and the Spanish dancer on black velvet and Hilary's latest happy news, if she was there, of the Alpha course. She wasn't there, probably out laughing it up with some happy-clappy Jesus crowd. My room looked small, the way childhood rooms look when you come back to them as a grown-up. There was *Hope* on the wall. I bought that print after Troy broke my nose and I moved out. Pathetic.

I had a shower, put on fresh jeans and a sweatshirt, thought about going to Phil's place, then decided not to just yet. I put on a jacket and went out to look for *Hope of a Tree*. WH Smith didn't have it so I went back to the Fulham Road and over to Nomad where I bought the one copy they had. 'How has this been selling?' I asked.

'We had two copies,' said the woman at the till. 'Sold the other one a couple of weeks ago.'

I didn't want to go directly home so I went past the North End Road to Caffè Nero at the corner of Vanston Place. It was busy but I got myself an

Americano and found an empty table by the window where I could start *Hope of a Tree* while drinking my coffee. The day was sunny and the Fulham Road was thronged with people doing their Saturday things. With my book and my coffee I felt as if I was in a little island of no hurry and no bother where I could let my mind be quiet for a while.

I opened the book. The dedication was *To the memory of my father, J. B. Ockerman*. The epigraph was from Job 14: 7:

> For there is hope of a tree, if it be cut
> down, that it will sprout again, and that
> the tender branch thereof will not cease.

Well, I thought, that's optimistic. Then I started chapter 1 and there's Cynthia on Clifton Bridge thinking about jumping and here comes Sam to talk her out of it. OK, I thought, you can get a good love story out of a beginning like that. Then I noticed a woman who'd just sat down at the next table watching me. She was about my age, not bad looking, maybe a little too much jaw, dark brown hair in a Louise Brooks cut. Black polo neck, little pink leather jacket, black trousers and Birkenstock. Very sleek, very cool and sure of herself.

She gave me a sort of knowing leer and said, 'Enjoying it?'

'Just started it,' I said. 'Have you read it?'

'Had to,' she said. 'I was married to the author.'

'Oh,' I said.

'Do you know him?' she said.

'Sort of,' I said. 'I'm his girlfriend.' I was surprised to hear myself say that but I tend to take against sleek women on sight.

'Really!' she said. 'He usually goes for the intellectual type. Which you don't, at first glance, appear to be.'

'It could be that he's looking to change his luck,' I said.

'Which way?' she said.

I stood up and took half a step towards her. She suddenly looked less sure of herself. 'Maybe,' I said. 'You'd like to continue this discussion outside?'

'Oh dear,' she said. 'Phil has come a long way down the female evolutionary ladder. This conversation would seem to be at an end. I suggest that you go back to your book and I to my cappuccino.'

'While you still have your teeth,' I said. She stayed quiet then, and when she picked up her cup it rattled in the saucer. I was amazed at my behaviour and quite pleased with it. Ms Ex-Wife finished her cappuccino quickly and left, avoiding eye contact the whole time.

I sat there with my book but I wasn't reading it; I was thinking about what I'd said: 'I'm his girlfriend.' Just like that. It's funny how you can have something in your mind but not know it until you hear yourself say it. So that was it – I was Phil's girlfriend. One more thing for me to deal with. Not simple. I wasn't sure I *wanted* to be Phil's girlfriend. I imagined the two of us walking down the street; did we look like a couple? Yes? No? OK, I thought, I'll go see him but first I'll read some more of his book.

Sam talks Cynthia down off the bridge and they go to the camera obscura. 'It's a dark chamber,' says Sam, 'but you get a clear bright view of things from here.' I imagined him saying that in the kind of film where you can see what's coming long before it arrives. Sam – he's American – would be played by Jim Carrey without his usual gurning and pretty soon we'd find out in a flashback that he'd been contemplating suicide after being dumped by Jennifer, played by Emily Watson. Cynthia would be Kate Winslet. An American film shot on location here.

'Another dark chamber?' says Cynthia as they start taking their clothes off at Sam's place on page 17. They get through the sex pretty quickly because that part is only foreplay for a whole lot of talk about books and music and painting and movies. With quotes from here and there in italics. Italics always tire me out. I had a second Americano because I was getting sleepy. Then I got up and walked down to the New King's Road and over to the river. I found myself a bench in Bishop's Park and sat there in the sunshine watching a crew rowing down the river with the cox yelling at them. For a while I just sat there trying to let my mind go blank but the book was in my hands and I kept thinking, Am I this guy's *girlfriend*? It's always a bad sign when you start thinking in italics. I read a little more but by then I knew I wasn't sure I could finish the book, it was too boring.

So where are we then? I thought. Am I his girlfriend because I feel that he needs me? Women who try to save drunks or gays hardly ever straighten them out. Was I going to be a boring-writer-saver? Phil's wife told him he was a failure when she divorced him. I pictured her saying that, sneerer that she was. Maybe she brought out the failure in him — that could happen with a guy like Phil. Could I bring out the non-failure? Did I even want to? I spun around a couple of times deciding whether to head for Phil's place or mine, then I shook my head and went home.

Back at the flat I breathed in the stale air and saw Hilary's Bible on the coffee table in the living room. I picked it up and it fell open to John, 11. My eye went to Verse 43:

> And when he thus had spoken, he
> cried with a loud voice, Lazarus,
> come forth.

'Jesus,' I said, 'gimme a break.' Then I thought I'd better check Phil's novel again to see if there were signs of life. I made myself a coffee, put on *The Essential Billie Holiday*, and settled down to carry on with Cynthia and Sam.

Cynthia is tall and blonde; Sam is short and dark. No surprises there. Cynthia is an assistant editor at the

Raven Press; Sam is a painter. Cynthia's contemplating suicide because she's been dumped by the man she's been with for two years and Sam is still emotionally entangled with his wife who killed herself three years ago. Of course Sam talks her down off the bridge and pretty soon they're sleeping together regularly but they don't enjoy it all that much – they're both holding on to the past and they can't let go of the bad experiences they've had. The story drags along with a lot of moaning and groaning on both sides until finally the two of them are on Clifton Bridge again looking down into the Avon Gorge but they don't jump. They decide to go their separate ways and search for new roots elsewhere. I wished they *had* jumped. So there I was back at the question of whether or not I wanted to be a boring–writer–saver. He wasn't boring to talk to and he wasn't a boring lover but still . . . Come to think of it, Brian was a better painter now than he'd been before he took up with me.

I needed a holiday from thoughts about Phil. If I went to Cheyne Walk Brian would be glad to see me and I was sure he'd put Cheryl on hold for as long as I stayed. So I left the flat, went to Fulham Broadway, caught an 11 bus, then walked from the King's Road.

I rang the bell, Brian buzzed me in and I went up to the studio. The floor was littered with Conté crayon sketches of Cheryl and she was on the model stand when I came into the room. 'Hi,' said Brian. To Cheryl he said, 'That's it for today. I'm not sure how I'm fixed for next week – I'll call you.' Cheryl nodded, got dressed, kissed him goodbye, and left. 'Old friends are the best friends,' said Brian as he grabbed my arse.

Later, with our clothes scattered on the floor, we sat in the studio without turning on the lights and watched the evening on the river. The lights on the Albert Bridge, the lights on passing boats and the look of the darkening sky all seemed as if I'd seen them before from this window. ' "*Some things that happen for the first time, Seem to be happening again . . .*" ' I sang softly.

Brian took my hand and kissed it, then he ordered up pizza and we drank almost two bottles of Chianti and fell asleep feeling well satisfied. No heavy thinking, just good clean fun.

Sunday, after a late breakfast and a lazy time with the papers, Brian got me out of my clothes again for some serious work. He tore off a large sheet from a big roll of brown wrapping paper and pinned it to a cork board which he put up on the easel.

'I haven't seen that before,' I said.

'I'm going to work with brush and ink and casein paint,' he said. 'It helps me to loosen up.'

I did twenty-minute poses and we worked for an hour before I rested. Brian had put up a new sheet of brown paper for each pose, so there were three of them lying on the floor. They were nothing like the Conté sketches he'd done of Cheryl; they were big and free but at the same time quite delicate. Full of tenderness, really, and the most sensitive nudes he'd ever done. 'These are beautiful,' I said. 'They're so different from your drawings of Cheryl.'

'Are you surprised?' he said, looking at me with his good eye foremost. Hearing what was in his voice I backed away a little and said, 'Better not.'

'Better not what?' he said.

'Get serious.'

'Why not? My feelings can't be that much of a surprise to you.'

Those were almost the same words he'd used when he'd tried to rape me the first time I posed for him. 'Stop right there,' I said. 'Put your heart back in your pants or I'm out of here.'

Brian found it hard to believe that I was rejecting his love. 'Can you do better?' he said. Always the pragmatist.

'Maybe I already have,' I said. I gathered up my clothes, got dressed and left.

7

PHIL OCKERMAN

I hadn't done anything but talk to Constanze – although I'd have liked to do more – and I'd no reason at all to feel guilty; in any case Barbara was shacked up with another man and for all I knew I might never see her again. But I *did* feel guilty, I felt that I had betrayed my density woman. Destiny woman. Both words are formed with the same letters and density is a big part of destiny. Your mind takes hold of something and it can feel whether the fabric is dense or thin: books, movies, music – anything. People.

Troy Wallis was much in my mind. In my youth I'd walked away from more fights than I'd taken on but I couldn't walk away from this one indefinitely. There was the Louisville Slugger leaning in the corner, tangible proof of my commitment – to myself as much as to Barbara. What if I'd never see her again? It seems I didn't really believe that. Courage was wanted from me, heroism even. Had I ever in my life done anything heroic? I'd once confronted three teenage louts who were making very noisy lewd remarks in the Chelsea Odeon while Mimi and I were there to see *Interview with the Vampire*. When I told them they were spoiling the film for the rest of us I got a blast of four-letter words and threats. 'OK,' I said. 'You're so tough, let me have your names so I'll know who you are.'

More verbal abuse followed this. 'We'll see you outside later,' said the senior lout. But they were quiet after that and they left before the end of the film. 'What are you going to do if they're waiting out there?' said Mimi as we left. 'I'll try to look like a figure of authority,' I said. But they weren't waiting. My bluff had apparently convinced them that I *was* a figure of authority. But that wasn't real heroism. I'd been reading about Nelson and the Battle of Trafalgar and I imagined those great wind-driven wooden fortresses coming slowly downwind through the French line: HMS *Victory*, *Temeraire*, *Royal Sovereign* and the others moving towards the moment when the marksman in the mizzen top of the *Redoutable* would aim for the stars on Nelson's coat. Nelson had to display himself in full regalia on the quarterdeck when the battle was at its height – that was part of what made him an inspiration to his men. At the age of eleven, considering his career prospects and the lack of any useful connections, he had written, 'Well then, I will be a hero, and confiding in Providence I will brave every danger.' But his crew above and below decks, men with no stars on their coats, many of them shirtless as they served their guns – they were too busy for displays; it was simply their job to be heroic, even the powder monkeys who might never reach puberty: there was nothing else to be, and in the heat of battle they were hooked up with the necessary violence in them, that practical violence that I'd never reached in myself.

I needed to walk the decks of HMS *Victory*. I needed to touch with my hands those great guns; I needed to stand in the orlop deck at the place where Nelson died. A visit to Portsmouth was what I needed. HMS *Victory* might seem a long way from the crypt at St James's Clerkenwell, even farther away from seventeenth-century Venice and Barbara Strozzi but, seen from Mercury and Venus as they look down on us, nothing is far away from anything.

On a dull and sultry day in July I went to Waterloo and took a South West train to Portsmouth Harbour. I seem to run into that kind of day when I'm looking for some hard-to-find thing, like a left-handed monkey wrench or whatever. After being nowhere for a while the train found Guildford. Then gradually the views on both sides became fields and trees and the sky seemed to widen. Time moved slowly and was further slowed down by the many mothers who were patiently reading to their children, playing games with them and feeding them snacks. The buffet car sent its nice little earner through the carriages with many kinds of overpriced refreshment but I'd brought my sandwich and bottle of water with me and was able to resist when the trolley paused for me.

Haslemere and other stations unrolled before and behind in due course while I read a book about *Bellerophon*, the seventy-four-gun ship of the line in Nelson's fleet known as *Billy Ruffian* to the sailors. Designed by Thomas Slade who also laid down the lines for HMS *Victory*, she was built in 1782 in the yard of Edward Greaves at Frindsbury in the River Medway in Kent. I'd received this book from a friend, and having nothing on HMS *Victory* I made do with the smaller vessel. More than three thousand oak trees were cut down to make the frames, strakes, beams, carlings, masts, yards and spars that with axe, saw, adze and drawknife were shaped and assembled into *Billy Ruffian*.

After my lunch I dozed off for a while and awoke when the train pulled into Petersfield. The sky was heavying up in a brooding sort of way and I had no doubt that its intentions were serious. Time now speeded up a little and Portsmouth Harbour was achieved, flaunting a vertical blot on the seascape that was clearly commissioned by one of those committees that can't leave anything alone. I learned later that it's called the Spinnaker Tower.

When I came out of the station I expected to see or at least hear gulls wheeling over the harbour but there were none. It was a half-mile or so from the railway station to HMS *Victory*, past HMS *Warrior*, various naval buildings, small craft moored in the harbour and a succession of eateries, boat-ride docks and other tourist attractions barnacled on to the dockyard along with a pub whose name I don't remember, the Royal Naval Museum and a shop that sold HMS *Victory* books, videos, and every kind of souvenir that England could expect. It was raining by then as it usually does when I'm looking for a left-handed monkey wrench or heroic inspiration.

Having bought my ticket I walked on glistening cobbles, along with the world and his camera, wife and children, towards the masts and rigging of Nelson's flagship which became gradually larger in our eyes as we approached. A life-size effigy of Nelson, a flat thing made of painted sheet metal, encouraged us to continue yet another half-mile or so to the queue waiting at the entrance to the ship.

HMS *Victory* is a three-decker 104-gun warship and it's huge. I'd never seen anything so big made out of wood by human hands. No power tools, just tools made by hand and worked by hand. When my ticket was punched I was given a printed guide. I have an in-grained resistance to manuals and guides, so I just followed the crowd up the gangway and into the lower gun deck. I have a problem with seeing things: when I go to an exhibition of paintings I clock the pictures briefly but I don't really study them, don't properly get *into* them until I look at the reproductions in the catalogue at home and recall to life the images recorded by my mind. So now in HMS *Victory*'s lower gun deck I trudged by dim lanterns past the thirty-two-pounder guns and their tackle, the rammers, sponges and the hammocks slung above them, all of our many tourist feet treading the planks where men long dead had walked and run and fallen. I couldn't see anything or feel anything, there was no privacy in which to see and feel.

Up and down steep stairs and companionways we went and at some point stood numerously in the orlop deck in front of the place where Nelson died. There was the oaken knee against which he leant as he lay dying. By it stood the painting of that scene by A. W. Devis. To the right was a painted wreath around the words, 'HERE NELSON DIED'. The lighting was too bright, it magnified the absence that prevailed. Foolishly I had hoped to feel Nelson's heroic death at the moment of victory but I felt only my own emptiness. You can buy a ticket to walk up and down and all around HMS *Victory* but the moment of Nelson's death is not for sale.

Still we kept trudging, and after a while the world and his camera, wife, children and I stood on the quarter deck. 'This is where Nelson was shot,' said an American voice, 'by a marksman in the rigging of the *Redoubtable*.'

'*Le Redou*table,' I said.'Mizzen top.' No one seemed to hear me. 'HERE NELSON FELL, 21st Oct 1805,' said the brass plaque.

On the way out I passed the great cabin and the stern lights through which Nelson must often have looked at the wake of his passage in all weathers. Now they showed today's grey rainlight that gleamed on his table, his telescope and sextant.

Then I was out in the rain again. At the shop I bought a book on HMS *Victory* and a video tour of the ship. I walked back to the station and in a short time was on a train back to London. I closed my eyes and waited for delayed heroic inspiration. What came to me, dark and shadowy, were the frames and timbers I had seen in the hold. These were of oak, their forms heroically achieved by the concerted skills of men with axes, saws, adzes, drawknives and augers who shaped them into the structure that would be planked up as the flagship of the fleet. The beautiful drawings in the book showed the lines, the framing, planking, masting, yards and spars of the ship they had built. Englishmen now alive had in their genes the army of skills that had flourished in this English nation.

Two hundred years ago my people, the Jews, had no nation. Their skills were scattered throughout the diaspora. In Biblical times there were Jews who built ships and sailed them: Hiram shipped ivory, apes and peacocks to Solomon from Ophir. There were Jews on the sea and by the sea, working in Akko, Joppa and other ports. Jesus's disciples were mainly Jewish fishermen who got their living in boats. But in my genes there was no army of Jews with axes, saws, adzes, drawknives and augers two hundred years ago.

I sat there in a funk for a certain time, then there came to mind Martin Buber's books on the Hasidim.

Aha! I said, and smote my forehead (one or two people looked at me): there are ships and ships; there is a great unsinkable oak-ribbed copper-bottomed ship of the mind, strong to weather any storm and impervious to all broadsides. Who built this ship? The zaddikim! Theirs the axes, the adzes, the augers, the strength of arm for the great unsinkable ship of the mind.

Who were these men? Rabbi Israel Ben Eliezer, the Baal Shem Tov! Dov Baer of Mezritch, the Great Maggid! Pinhas of Koretz and his school, yes! Such as these and other illustrious zaddikim were the men. Swarming up the rigging, they manned the yards and stood ready. With them behind me and the Louisville Slugger ready to hand I felt that I could deal with whatever had to be dealt with.

But as I was putting the zaddikim back on the shelf Rabbi Moshe Leib slipped out and said,

To know the needs of another and to bear the burden of their sorrow, that is the true love.

'We weren't talking about love, Moshe,' I said. 'And besides, Troy Wallis is a big sorrow for Barbara and I'm bearing the burden like a true lover.'

'So you'll bash in his brains with your baseball bat, yes?'

'Strictly in self-defence.'

'Which means he'll have to attack you.'

'Or Barbara – the way it was in *The Rainmaker*.'

'And what, he'll also have a baseball bat?'

'He doesn't need one, he's very big and very strong – he's a professional bouncer. I'll have to play it by ear and see how the situation develops.'

'It sounds to me like a disaster waiting to happen.'

'So tell me, Rabbi Moshe, from the depths of your wisdom, what should I do?'

'Who knows? Sometimes a disaster is just something you have to get out of your system.'

'With this kind of advice you became famous?'

'I came off the shelf to talk to you about true love and sorrow, not baseball bats, OK? Your first priority is Barbara's sorrow.' And with that he was gone.

8

BARBARA STRUNK

I was going to phone Phil before I left for work but then I didn't; it was one of those times when I wasn't exactly depressed but I was anxious and scared and sad: I didn't know where I was with Phil and I didn't know where I was in myself. Is the world real? I wondered. What is this that's looking out of my eyes? 'Never mind,' I heard myself say. 'Time to go to work.'

As always, I took the District Line to Notting Hill Gate where I changed to the Central Line. When I came out at Oxford Circus the ordinary rhythm of a July Thursday seemed to have been disrupted. Some people were walking quickly and looking anxious; others stood in little knots and talked with many gestures. Listening to them I learned that there had been bombs in the Underground. I tried to ring Phil on my mobile but the network had been shut down.

When I got to the Lichtheim brothers they had the radio on with all the details: three bombs in the Underground and one in a bus; many dead and injured and the Underground system was now shut down. I phoned Phil on the landline and got his answering machine. 'Are you all right?' I said. 'Call me at work!' then I thought that he might be out doing one of his workshops and not near a phone. Maybe in a tube train.

I was enraged by the bombings. I flung my arm out as if to push away this intrusion; how dared they do this to my London! Then as details kept pouring in my mind filled with the screams of the wounded and the panic of those climbing over bodies to walk the tracks in darkness. And more dead and injured in the double-decker bus that stood in the sunlight by Russell Square with its top blown off. My hands were shaking so badly that I couldn't do anything with artificial eyes so Karl told me to go home. The sunny day was a mockery and the ordinariness of a London Thursday was gone. It was as if London was an anthill that had been kicked by a giant foot; there was nothing gigantic about the bombers, they were just creeps with evil minds. It was Terror that was the giant: Here I am, it said. I have always been here but now you will pay attention.

It was too early in the day for drinking but I badly wanted a drink. I headed for The Blue Posts knowing they'd be closed but hoping for sanctuary from the weirdness of the day. When I got there I found Grace Kowalski looking at the closed doors and shaking her head. 'I know it's too early,' she said, 'but I feel like drinking and I don't want to do it alone.'

'Bombers evidently can't disturb the British licensing laws,' I said.

'Never mind,' she said. 'Come up to my place and we'll do early drinking not alone.'

The baseball bat in its velvet sheath was slung from her shoulder as before. 'I see that Irv is with you,' I said.

'Always.'

'I hope some day to hear Irv's history.'

'I don't know,' said Grace. 'It's a matter of how much disbelief you can suspend. Do you work out?'

'No. Why?'

'Suspending enough disbelief to believe Irv's history would be roughly equivalent to pressing four hundred pounds.'

'Maybe I could suspend a little each day and gradually work my way up to the full whack.'

'We'll see,' said Grace. The shop was closed; we went up the stairs to the studio. The place smelled of soldering and unknown chemicals. On the workbench were coils of brass and silver wire, various small pliers and cutters, and boxes filled with bits of coloured glass. In the vice was an unfinished angel brooch, brilliantly bejewelled. On the workbench lay a goat done in yellow, orange and brown glass. It was a longhaired goat like the one in the William Holman Hunt painting.

'Scapegoat?' I said.

'Right,' said Grace.

'Odd thing for someone to wear.'

'I have odd customers.'

'There's a verse in Leviticus that tells how Aaron put all the iniquities and sins of the children of Israel on the head of the goat and drove it out into the wilderness.'

'To Azazel,' said Grace, 'the demon of the desert.'

'So who's ordered this goat?'

'I'm not at liberty to say. But there are a lot of deserts about, and where there's a desert you'll find Azazel. Drink is next on the programme: all I have is vodka.'

'Didn't you say that the ravages of time had forced you to switch to beer?'

'I lied,' she said. She went to the fridge and took a bottle of Stolichnaya from the freezer. She poured two glasses and we clinked. 'Here's looking at you,' said Grace.

'Here's looking right back.' The cold vodka went down my neck beautifully, and after the third glass it seemed the icy blast of pure reason. 'Your bat's named after one some,' I said. 'Someone.'

Grace nodded. 'Irv Goodman. Fell in love too late.'

'With you?'

'With me. He was eighty-three.'

'Ah.'

'We were both in the nick and he got pneumonia and died a week after they let us go.'

'I'm sorry. Why were you in the nick?'

'DI Hunter didn't believe what we told him and he was pissed off so he locked us up.'

'What did you tell him?'

'You wouldn't believe it either.'

'Anything to do with vumpires, ampires?'

'Maybe, but not the usual kind – there's a batrachian elephant, element.'

'What's a batrachian elephant?'

'Frogs and toads. Am I making myself queer?'

'Transparently but can leave it for another time. Now think I'll go home and have little lie-down.'

Getting home wasn't easy – the Underground was shut down and taxis were not to be had. I walked for a long time and then stood by the curb looking hopeful and was finally picked up by a man on a red Yamaha who lived in Hammersmith and chivalrously dropped me at my door.

I got there just in time for a throw-up before the lie-down. Up came breakfast and vodka, the bombs in the Underground and bus, the dead and the injured, my morning sadness and everything else.

I slept until almost five, realised I didn't know if Phil was all right, and rang him up. I got his answering machine and left a message for him to phone me. Then I made a coffee and waited for the phone to ring. After the third cup it rang. 'Barbara,' said Phil, 'are you all right?'

'I'm OK. I was nowhere near any explosions. What about you?'

'I'm OK. It's a surreal kind of day and I haven't really taken it in yet. I'm at Euston, about to leave for Scotland.'

'How come?'

'I'm tutoring a writing course at Diamond Heart – it's near Port Malkie on the Moray Firth. I didn't know about it until this morning – the guy who was scheduled to do it is off sick so they called me.'

'How long will you be gone?'

'A week – it's a residential thing. The course I'm taking over is "The Search for Page One".'

'I hope you find it. How is it with all those people living together up there?'

'It's about what you'd expect – people talk bollocks, get laid, and do a little writing that I have to read and help them with.'

'Do the women tend to need a lot of help?'

'Depends on the tutor. Ken Hackett who was meant to do the course is a good-looking guy with a high scoring average.'

'What about you?'

'This time I'll confine my tutoring to talking bollocks. But no sex.'

'You're giving it up for Yom Kippur?'

'I don't want to weaken the connection.'

'What connection is that?'

'The one between you and me.'

Pause.

'Barbara?'

'I'm here. I was letting your words linger in my ear.'

'Ah, that's nice. I have to go now, I'll phone you when I get there.'

'Don't phone – I'd like a week where we can walk around in each other's minds and listen to each other without telephones.'

'OK. If I say anything good, write it down. I'm off, see you in a week.'

'See you.'

I was thinking about that connection between us, wondering if it was like the string between two tin-can telephones. I sat there with my finger in my navel for a while, then I went into the kitchen to make some coffee.

Hilary was sitting there with a cup of tea and her Bible. 'How was *your* day?' I said. She's an estate agent with Vanston here in Fulham.

'"And I looked,"' she said, '"and behold a pale horse: and his name that sat on him was Death, and Hell followed with him." We closed early but some of the staff probably aren't home yet. There's an Alpha meeting tonight and I expect I'll be back later than usual.'

Her Bible remained on the kitchen table after she left, still open at Revelation 6. Hilary likes to do that, leave the open book where my eye might be caught by the Word of God. I'm impervious to it.

Back at work the next day I was wondering where the stars and planets stood with yesterday's bombings. *The Times* had star maps every month and the constellations drawn in white lines and dots on the black circle of July's night sky certainly seemed to be telling us something. Mercury and Venus were low in the north-west but there was nothing that interested me in the rest of the text.

At the studio I googled around and found *The Visual Astrology Newsletter*. '*Nergal claims the empty sky . . .*' was the first thing it said. I liked the sound of that so I read on. 'The sky has never stopped talking; rather we have stopped listening,' said Bernadette Brady, the writer of the newsletter. Using 'concepts discussed by the Chaldean priests of over 2,500 years ago' she claimed clear predictions of the death of the pope and London's successful Olympics bid.

Nergal is Mars, said Brady. She was into the astrological explanation of the bombings when I was sidetracked by that name. Where had I heard it before? I googled for it and found a website by Lishtar. In the Mesopotamian Underworld Ereshkigal is 'the inflexible goddess of the Land of No Return . . .' Such splendid names! And Nergal is 'the stubborn god of War and Pestilences'. I'd heard of those two in one of Brian's lectures and they'd just been names you hear in a lecture but now they grew big and pushed astrology to one side. 'Aha!' I said as it came to me that Ereshkigal and Nergal both lived in me and the two of them lived in Phil also and that's why nothing was simple.

On Saturday I craved the melancholy sunlight of Claude's paintings so I went to the National Gallery. I was stood in front of *The Embarkation of Saint Ursula*, taking in the sadness and goodbyeness of it, the blueness and farawayness of the Claudian waves that were like rollers cranked by stagehands, and remembering what Brian had said in another of his slide lectures. 'She took eleven thousand Christian virgins with her on a pilgrimage to Rome and on the way back they were all slaughtered by the Huns. I call that a terrible waste of virginity.

'This subject was painted in the fourteenth century by Tommaso da Modena; in the fifteenth by Vittore Carpaccio and Hans Memling; and in the seventeenth by Claude. Tommaso gives us a William Morris sort of thing; Carpaccio offers a workmanlike and completely prosaic job with pretty costumes; Memling's version is compact and tidy with pleasantly chunky ships and people cleverly fitted into the space. But only in Claude do we find the great sadness of doomed innocence. The colours and the atmosphere are elegaic; the ships are ships of dreams; the virgins already have a sacrificial look. This picture says it all – the innocence of mortal life embarking always on its deathward voyage.'

'This world is not a safe place for virgins, is it?' said the woman who had joined me and Claude. It was Mimi, Phil's ex.

'It's not safe for anyone,' I said. She was wearing the brooch that I'd seen on Grace Kowalski's workbench. 'What's that in aid of?' I asked.

'Do you know what it is?'

'It's a scapegoat.'

'That's me,' she said. 'My ID.'

'Why is that?'

'Doesn't Phil blame me for his failure?'

'*Is* he a failure?'

'Did you ever finish *Hope of a Tree*?'

'Yes, I did.'

'Well done you! What's your opinion of it?'

'It's not the most exciting thing I've ever read but that doesn't make Phil a failure. In any case, whatever he is, he's out of your life now and you can move on.'

'Nobody you've been married to for twelve years is ever completely out of your life,' she said. A wistful note there?

'And now you want him back?'

'No, but I can't help wondering how he's doing under new management. Would you say that you inspire him?'

'I don't manage him, and the rest is none of your business. Whether you're being a dog in the manger or a bitch in heat I'd be delighted if we could agree not to be friends and if you could just bugger off.'

After she'd gone I found myself thinking Brian thoughts. Remembering the times we'd had, the things we'd done. He'd asked me if I could do better and I'd said that maybe I already had. Still, when he wasn't in courtship mode he was very easy to be with and I didn't have to break my head trying to work out what we were to each other. Simple is what everybody wants but very few of us get.

9

PHIL OCKERMAN

Max Lesser has some time ago described Diamond Heart [See *Her Name Was Lola*, Bloomsbury, 2003] and with his permission we borrow from it for the present narrative. 'Diamond Heart,' says the brochure, 'is not a retreat. It is a centre of dynamic calm in which mind and spirit gather energy for the next forward move. On offer are Yoga, Tai Chi, Feng Shui, and Zen disciplines including meditation, gardening, flower arrangement, archery, snooker, and poker. Vegetarian, Kosher, and Halal cuisine. Acupuncture, Reflexology, Aromatherapy, and homeopathic medicine. Tuition in classical Indian music with Hariprasad and Indira Khan. This year we have added writing courses which will be tutored by established novelists, playwrights and poets.'

Diamond Heart has given a new lease of life to the defunct herring port of Port Mackie on the Firth of Moray. The harbour is almost empty, stretching out its arms to the past. The tide comes in, goes out around

Kirsty's Knowe, Teeny Titties and Deil's Hurdies. The wind sighs in the grasses. The pebbles rattle in the tidewash, the sea-shapen rocks abide. There are plenty of gulls, shags, and cormorants but no herring. Port Mackie now buzzes with new businesses supplying goods and services to Diamond Heart.

Diamond Heart is not cheap. The one thing its varied clientele have in common is that they can all afford it. There are ageing hippies, youthful rebels, stressed-out executives, ex-husbands and ex-wives, broken-down pop stars, actors between (sometimes for years) engagements, and various unemployed of independent means. Cannabis and cocaine are not compulsory. The Diamond Heart complex is made up of dome-shaped buildings (called *tholoi* in the brochure) overlooking the sea. It has the added attraction of its own myths and legends of which more later.

There were nine people in my group: four men and five women. Three of the women were chronic course-takers with hopeful smiles and it's-so-nice-to-be-here expressions. The fourth looked dead serious and probably had two or three unpublished novels in her rucksack. The fifth was Constanze Webber. Two of the men looked like course-takers to me and the other two looked serious.

'Hi, Constanze,' I said. 'How's it going with the music?'

'Very slowly,' she said. 'I'd like to have a go at fiction for a change. I've got a couple of ideas for stories but I don't know how to get started.'

'I have the same problem,' said one of the serious men.

'Me too,' said one of the female course-takers. 'I have things in my head but when I try to put them down on paper I can't get past the first line.'

'That's what I'm here for,' I said.

'It said in the brochure that Ken Hackett would be doing "The Search for Page One",' said Constanze.

'He's got flu,' I said, 'but not to worry — there's nothing I don't know about searching for Page One.'

'What about finding it?' she said.

'Trust me,' I said. 'We might get lucky. The most common failing of the inexperienced writer is thinking that you have to begin at the beginning.'

'Where else would you begin?' said the dead-serious young woman whose bulging rucksack threatened many pages for me to read.

'Wherever the thing presents itself to you — the arse or the elbow or the foot. The raw material is showing you that because it's what you can bring everything out of by working backwards and forwards from it. Look at the opening of *Daniel Deronda* — it's not the chronological beginning of the novel; quite a few things have happened and most of the main characters have appeared in the story earlier but not on the page, so from that opening scene in the casino Eliot has to develop people and events around the psychological centre which is the action between Gwendolen Harleth and Daniel Deronda. Because that was the beginning.'

'*In media res,*' said she of the serious rucksack.

'Exactly,' I said. 'In the middle of things is where you often find the beginning.'

'How many ls in Eliot?' said one of the course-takers.

'One,' I said. 'What I'd like all of you to do now is to give me whatever you've brought with you so I can start reading. If you haven't brought anything you should write whatever you can for me to look at tomorrow. Don't demand too much of yourself – heavy expectations tend to be self-defeating.'

Those who had manuscripts passed them along to me while the others scratched their heads, looked around, and slowly put pen to paper. Constanze's was the last of the mss. It was a single sheet of blue A4 copy paper, somewhat crumpled. On it was printed a single line: '*"That's what uncles do," he said.*'

'Uncle Teddy?' I said as various of the group turned to look at me.

Constanze nodded. I put the page into a folder and picked up a thick wodge of paper from the dead-serious girl whose name was Clara Petersen. *Low Pressure Love* was the title. '*It rained whenever we met.*' was the first line. 'Listen to this,' I said to the group, and I read them the line. 'That right away pulls me in,' I said, 'because it rings true: there are times like that and there are lives like that. I want to read on and find out who the narrator is and what's coming next. I already care about the narrator and I want to get into the action. If your story doesn't engage the reader and make him or her want to know more you haven't got a story. It doesn't have to be a person that the reader is drawn in by: *Bleak House* opens with "implacable November weather", with mud and smoke and fog and you want to go where the weather is taking you because the writer has made you care by putting you into a place and an atmosphere of impending excitement.'

Some people nodded, others took notes, others did both. I refrained from launching into the first page of *Moby Dick* although damp drizzly Novembers are a regular feature of my internal climate and I asked Clara to read the whole first page of her ms to the group. It was a good Page One and I made good comments after the reading. The whole novella, which I read later, was excellent. Clara had talent and the necessary strength of character for the long haul and I told her I'd do my best to put her in touch with an agent. She was quite a good-looking girl too, very intense with her dark hair worn long and a *Wuthering Heights* air about her which would do nicely in jacket photos and book promotion. I couldn't help wondering what it would be like to live with her and I was glad I didn't. But now I'm going to leave Clara and the rest of the group in order to report my conversation with Constanze about Uncle Teddy. After supper I found her waiting for me. The summer evening was mild and the sound of the sea had a confidential air. *Secrets!* it whispered in the hissing of the waves on the strand, *Secrets! I hold them, I keep them.* There was a little thin sickle moon hanging in the clear sky. Lights glimmered all over Diamond Heart and a murmur of voices rose up with the smell of cannabis and the sound of an accordion and someone singing, in Russian, the song in which the English refrain begins with 'Those were the days, my friend . . .' We passed the Xanadu dome where the drinkers mostly stood outside and made pub noises.

'Where are we going?' I said.

'Kirsty's Knowe,' said Constanze. 'I like to go there to be quiet.' She took me to a grassy hill overlooking the sea where the susurrus of the waves made a whispering stillness that seemed to wait for something.

'What's it waiting for?' I asked her.

'Ah!' she said, 'you feel it too. This place is haunted. There was a Kirsty who hanged herself when her lover abandoned her. Kirsty's Fetch, her ghost is called, and men who see it are fated to be drowned. And they say if you go to the Deil's Hurdies you can hear the voices of the dead.'

'I don't see Kirsty's Fetch so far,' I said.

'I don't think you're destined to drown.'

'Are you going to write about Uncle Teddy?'

'I don't want to but that line jumped on to the paper and it's pulling me after it.'

'All of us have the ghosts of ourselves inside us,' I said. She turned to me and her five foot ten seemed smaller and unsure. Mostly she looked like a confident winner but now she was touchingly vulnerable – I wanted to cuddle her but it would have been a wrong move and unwanted as well. Moshe Leib's words recurred to me. 'There's a sorrow in you,' I said, 'just as there is in all of us. This sorrow clothes itself in various memories. I find it's best to let the thing get on to the paper. You can always tear it up later if you want to.'

Looking out into the sea-dark she said, 'He used to take me on his lap. Once, when I was ten, he put his hand . . .'

'Stop!' I said. 'Don't talk it out – get it down on paper and maybe it'll lead to something further.'

'All right,' she said. 'I'll start tonight then because ideas are coming to me right now. See you tomorrow.'

When we parted I watched her walk away and Moshe Leib's words about the burden of one's sorrow came to mind again. There's a lot of it about, I thought. Barbara's face came to me then, with her look of unknowing that was so characteristic of her. Perhaps it mirrored the look on my face? It's very difficult to know anything, really, and here I was teaching people as if I knew something they didn't. I was experienced in some ways – I was like a tracker who always found the turds of his prey but never caught the animal he was after. I stopped in at the Xanadu and ordered a large Glenfiddich.

One of the men in my group came up to me and nodded. I didn't remember his name. 'Geoff Wiggins,' he said. 'I'd like to write but I can't think of anything to write about.'

'Write about that then,' I said. 'If you do it carefully and honestly something will come to you.'

'Does that always work for you?' he said.

'Sure it does. What comes to me is crap a lot of the time but that's how it is.'

'I guess if you were more successful you wouldn't need to teach courses like this.'

'And if you were capable of sitting at a desk alone you wouldn't need to take courses like this,' I said.

We both smiled hard at each other and he walked away.

Hoping I wouldn't see any more familiar faces I had a look around me. Diamond Heart, definitely not a retreat, was a cruising ground offering interesting people of all sexual persuasions, most of them with a look of easy availability. It was rather like an auction where you had to be careful not to scratch your nose. It was the kind of scene I used to enjoy but now I found the whole thing dissolving into visual noise like a computer picture infected with a virus.

I had manuscripts to read but I put it off yet awhile. I finished my drink, went outside and walked back to Kirsty's Knowe. I sat down on the still-warm grass, closed my eyes and listened to the sea. The warm summer air seemed a medium of transmission and Barbara's face came to me then. I'd never been able to recall it accurately before but here it was utterly clear and real. I didn't think any words, just looked at her face while the sea whispered me its secrets. At the beginning of these pages I've given my first impression of her that Saturday night at St James's Clerkenwell. I described her as having a long oval face, a sullen mouth, and an up-yours expression. But attractive, I said: a face that pulled the eye. A *shapely* face that followed up the shapeliness of her legs and referred itself to the hidden sensuality of her body. As I looked at her now her face asserted its Strozzi attributes: the sombre eyes; the small mouth with its full underlip; the round chin that completed the juiciness of the mouth and led the eye down to the full breasts. Now my Barbara had become Barbara Strozzi and now the face flickered between the two of them, proclaiming the mystery of itself and the unknowability of Woman and sorrow. Tears rolled down my face; almost I could believe in God, or at least a demiurge. My empty hands moved as if kneading the dust of stars into wet clay. I looked up at the sky wondering what effect Mercury and Venus, all unseen, might be having on me.

Without being aware of having walked there I found myself at the guest dome where I was staying. Feeling strange but not sleepy I read Clara Petersen's novella and several of the short bits from the group. When I fell asleep I dreamed that Barbara Strozzi kissed me and put my hand on her breast.

Next morning Constanze arrived at the group session with the pages she'd written. First I gave my comments on Clara's ms, then I went through the short bits I'd read. I'm never brutal in my critiques but there's no escaping the fact that some would-be writers have it and some don't. Many of the people who take these courses have a modicum of talent but very few will ever be published because talent isn't enough: you need the character that will drive the talent as far as it can go.

'Are you going to read this out?' I said to Constanze.

'Yes,' she said, taking up a position at the front. 'This is the first chapter of a novel and the title is *Uncle William's Lap.*'

'You've been doing this to me since I was ten,' I said.

He smiled down at me while he took his pleasure. 'Well, love,' he said, 'this is what uncles do.'

'Not any more,' I said, and reached under the bed for the knife. We came together, then I cut short his enjoyment and a very messy business it was. After I'd dismembered the body and buried the pieces in different places far apart I burned the bedclothes, had a long hot shower, opened a bottle of Veuve Clicquot and thought about the last fifteen years.

She went on to read the whole first chapter which was five pages long, her South African accent adding a little something to the eroticism and the nastiness of it. When she stopped there was spontaneous applause from the coarser element of the group. 'Don't stop!' was their cry. 'Go for it! Give us more!' Clara shook her head sadly.

'That's all she wrote so far,' said Constanze, 'but I'll keep working on it.'

After supper I found her at the Xanadu surrounded

by admirers. 'What you read out today was quite different from your songwriting,' I said.

'The songs are my art,' she said. 'This is for money. Do you think I'll get it published?'

'Probably,' I said. 'Under your own name?'

'Why not?'

'Don't you feel at all strange about it?'

'Why should I? This is a legitimate commercial product — it's entertainment.'

'Yes, but the songs are a class act and this is something you'd be better off not putting your name to.'

'Are you applying to be my uncle now?'

'Why? Is the situation vacant?'

'Who knows? You might get lucky.' Gasps and giggles from her audience.

'Thank you but I'm fully committed elsewhere.'

'No problem. But tell me: Haven't you ever wanted to write something that wasn't boring?' The circle of admirers had backed off a little to give us space but now there were more gasps followed by bursts of laughter.

I felt a hot wave of anger rising in me but I tried to stay cool. 'What I write doesn't seem boring to me,' I said, 'and it takes up my whole self so there's nothing left over for any other kind of writing.'

'I think you might be a self-defeater, Teach. Maybe you should take up another line of work.' General tittering from the sidelines.

'Like what?'

'I don't know. Plumbing maybe. It's a useful trade, it gets you out of the house and plumbers make a lot of money.' She was swaying a little as she spoke. Evidently the drinks following on her popularity had somewhat gone to her head.

'Thanks for the advice,' I said. 'I appreciate your concern.'

'You're welcome. And I'll be there tomorrow with the rest of the swine to pick up any pearls you might be throwing our way.'

'I think you're going to have a hangover in the morning, so I'll wish you a good night now.'

'Goodnight, Uncle Not.' Accompanied by two or three well-wishers and the scent of cannabis she departed.

I walked out to Kirsty's Knowe again and waited for Barbara's face to come to me. It didn't come and I sat there asking myself how I could make ends meet without teaching.

Constanze didn't turn up the next morning. She left a note for me with Geoff Wiggins:

Dear Uncle Not,
I think it's best if I leave now. I'm too embarrassed – for you.

See you around. Or not.
Constanze

I finished the week somehow. It's nothing I feel like talking about. The group had an end-of-course party that I didn't go to. They gave me a bottle of plonk and I left it on the desk where they put it. On the train going home I did some arithmetic: if I didn't do any more teaching I had enough to live on for seven or eight months. What then? No idea. I trusted that something would come to me; it always had so far.

With that settled I was able to give my attention to Barbara. I closed my eyes and this time her face came to me with its beauty and its sorrow. It was there only for a moment before a shadow fell across it and there was Troy Wallis. There are things in life that compel recognition, things that you know are for you and nobody else. You can't get around them; you have to go through them or be stopped by them. I remembered how it was when Barbara and I watched *The Rainmaker*, how excited she was when Rudy was about to finish off Kelly's husband. '*Stop!*' said Kelly. '*Give me the bat. You were not here tonight. Go!*' And when Rudy left, she struck the final blow and Barbara hugged me and kissed me and asked if she could stay the night.

Lovely. But Barbara and I were not in a movie. However appealing the idea of duplicating that scene in real life, there was no practical way of making it happen. I couldn't see myself walking around with a baseball bat. Too big for a violin case. Double bass? Not exactly a quick-draw thing: Don't look now, Troy, I have a surprise for you. Barbara as bait? He follows her and I show up with the Louisville Slugger disguised as a French bread, upon which I do it to him before he does it to me. Right, no problem. Meanwhile there was the six-foot-four reality of him in front of Jimmy Maloney's like a wall.

I called Barbara as soon as I got back. 'Sometimes I can see you when I close my eyes and sometimes I can't,' I said.

'That's how it is with me too,' she said. 'I think the trick is not to try. When I look away mentally your face comes to me.'

'Did I say anything good while I was walking around in your head?'

'You hummed – tangoes. "La Cumparsa" seemed to be your favourite.'

'I wouldn't have thought you knew that one.'

'Grace Kowalski heard me humming it and she was surprised too.'

'It was made into a song with an English lyric,' I said: ' "For Want of a Star". "For want of a star a dream had to die, For want of a dream the stars left the sky . . ." That's all I remember.'

'That's a pretty sad song to carry around in your head.'

'Yes, it is. I guess sadness is my default setting.'

'Mine too. Maybe everybody's. What did I do when I was walking around in *your* head?'

'You were explaining something with all kinds of gestures but no words – you did it in absolute silence.'

'What was I explaining?'

'I never figured it out.'

'Shall I come to your place this evening?'

'That would be like rain on parched earth. This time I'll pick you up at your place and walk you to mine.'

'Very gentlemanly! Around seven?'

'See you then.'

At seven she came out when I knocked and I thought *My* woman! 'Wow!' I said. She was wearing a black T-shirt with a large Mickey Mouse in coloured sequins, a little denim skirt with a broad red leather belt slung low on her hips. The skirt was wider than the belt but not much. The rest was bare legs ending in roman sandals with straps halfway up the calf. Looking at her legs I said, 'Thank you, God.' She laughed and we kissed. 'Glad to see me?' she said.

'If I were a bell I'd be ringing,' I answered. 'Nothing less than champagne will do this evening. We can get it at Waitrose.' We crossed to the other side of the North End Road and found ourselves face to face with Troy Wallis. As if he'd sprung out of the ground.

He grabbed Barbara by the arms and began to shake her. I moved in and said, 'No more of that! She's with me now!'

'Jesus, Bertha,' he said, 'is this the best you can do?' With his right arm he knocked me down with a backhand blow. Before I could get up he kicked me but I managed to grab his foot and pull. He fell backward and his head hit the pavement, Wham! He lay flat on his back absolutely still with a pool of blood spreading under his head. Barbara was laughing hysterically. 'Stop!

Give me the bat,' she said. 'You were not here tonight. Go!'

I put my arm around her shoulders and urged her to pull herself together. A middle-aged couple had seen the whole thing and they came to where we stood looking down at Troy.

'I'm a nurse,' said the woman. She bent down and felt for Troy's pulse. She shook her head. 'He's dead,' she said. I dialled 999 on my mobile and we stood there waiting for the police and an ambulance to arrive.

Barbara was shaking her head in astonishment. Looking from Troy to me she said, 'He picked the wrong guy to fuck with – I guess it was bound to happen some time.'

'You might say it was an occupational hazard in his line of work,' I said.

'In movies,' said Barbara, 'when a non-violent man kills somebody the way you just did, he turns away and vomits but you didn't.'

'Nothing to vomit about, all men are violent – it's just that not all of us can act it out.'

'Now that he's dead I feel sort of dropped. What do we do now, live happily ever after? How do we get from here to what comes next?'

'We'll just have to work at it: if we can't get under it we'll have to get over it.'

'Why would we want to get under it?'

'I don't know – it's a Hasidic thing.' By this time the police and the ambulance had arrived with sirens and flashing lights and a small crowd quickly gathered. 'What happened?' said those in the rear to those in front.

'There was a fight over a woman,' came the answer.

'Who won?'

'The one that's talking to the cop.'

There were a PC and a WPC on the scene. The police of course have less money to spend than the networks and the WPC didn't look as good as the ones on TV. She took a Polaroid of the body and drew a chalk outline around it. The PC spoke briefly into his radio, then turned to us. 'Who called this in?' he said.

'I did,' I said.

'Your name please,' said the PC.

I told him and he wrote it down. 'Who's the deceased?' he said. When I'd given him Troy's name he said, 'Who are these other people?'

'I'm the wife of the deceased,' said Barbara. 'Widow, actually. But we weren't living together any more.'

'What about you, Mr Ockerman?' he said. 'What was your relation to Troy Wallis?'

'None.'

'How'd you get the black eye?'

'He knocked me down and tried to kick me but I grabbed his foot and he fell backwards and struck his head on the pavement.'

'Why did he knock you down?'

'Because I was with Ms Strunk.'

'My husband and I witnessed the whole thing,' said the nurse.

'Right,' said the PC. To the paramedics he said, 'You can take the body to the morgue. There's no question about the time and cause of death – I'll call the ME.' To the crowd he said, as Troy's feet disappeared into the ambulance, 'Let's move on, people, there's nothing more to see.' To the rest of us he said, 'We're going to need statements from all of you, so if you'd like to step around the corner to the police station we'll get that done.'

We followed him and the WPC to the street behind Waitrose and the blue lamps and steps of the station. By this time I was feeling the after-effects of the evening's action and my impressions were somewhat blurred. I think there were various notices on the walls and photos of persons wanted for one thing and another. Although the lighting was probably adequate the place had a one-eyed blinking sort of look (which may have been due to the closure of my left eye from Wallis's backhander). Two PCs were supporting a drunk while the duty sergeant at the desk took down the details of what I gathered was his attempted assault on the two officers. 'Name?' said the sergeant.

'Mickey Mouse,' said the drunk.

Barbara and I and the nurse and her husband had our details taken down and made our statements, after which I was arrested as a murder suspect by the duty sergeant, had the contents of my pockets listed and bagged, and was taken to a cell. 'See you tomorrow,' said Barbara as she kissed me goodnight. I lay down on the bed and sank into a restless sleep in which I dreamed that Troy kept jumping up as fast as I killed him.

In the morning the sky was flat and grey and I was taken to the West London Magistrates Court in Talgarth Road. The magistrate reduced the charge to manslaughter and my case went to the Old Bailey for trial at the first available court date. I was then released on £10,000 bail. 'Who put up the ten thousand?' I asked. 'Name withheld,' said the bondsman. I was released pending a hearing. After that, as I had a permanent address, no record, and wasn't on any other wanted list the magistrate said I could go home.

Barbara came to meet me. As we walked to my place together I thought of the virgin Louisville Slugger leaning in its corner. 'Oh God,' I said.

'Oh God what?'

'I don't want to say it.'

'Say it.'

'What if . . .?'

'What if what?'

'What if our whole relationship has only been held together by the prospect of killing your husband? Would you have stayed with me otherwise?'

'Oh shit, I'm not sure of anything any more. What do we do now?'

'I don't know – my place? Pizza?'

'OK. I don't really want to make any decisions.'

We went to Basuto Road walking like zombies. When the pizza arrived we ate it and drank beer without saying much, and afterwards Barbara went straight to bed.

I rang up Catriona. 'Please,' I said, 'tell me how things are looking for me.'

'Well,' she said, 'your Moon is opposed by Pluto and there's possible action pending from dangerous females. If you aren't dangerous enough yourself, you and your female might drift apart. Maybe that would even be desirable to one or both of you. Things are looking dodgy, so watch your arse.'

'Dangerous females!' I said. 'What other kind is there?'

IO

BARBARA STRUNK

OK, I love him or so it seems. But is love enough? Do I want to spend the rest of my life with a guy who writes boring? I'm trying not to be a talent snob but I'm not sure he's got what it takes to come up with an interesting book. Sticking with him through weeks and months and years of boring would be really heavy work. When I rejected Brian and he asked me if I could do better I said, 'Maybe I already have.' But *have* I? Brian has talent and he's getting better all the time. He's fun to be with and he makes me feel good. I like the kind of person he is and he likes the kind of person I am. That can't be bad, can it? He's taller than I am too.

I was thinking these thoughts (and feeling guilty) as I lay in bed with Phil beside me. I could tell by his breathing that he wasn't asleep either. I was still awake when the Underground started running and the room got light. I guess we both got some sleep then, and around seven Phil got up, went to the bathroom, showered and got dressed.

I followed him, and in due course we appeared in the kitchen, kissed each other good morning in a small way, and had orange juice, toast and marmalade and coffee. 'Let's eat out tonight,' said Phil.

'OK,' I said. 'See you,' and left for work.

The studio was always a cosy place and this morning's music was Emmylou Harris but the eye I was painting was giving me a cold and fishy stare and I felt shut off from the world. At lunchtime I went to The Blue Posts hoping to see Grace Kowalski and there she was with Irv and a half of Directors. 'Hi,' I said. 'Have you posed for Brian yet?'

'Yup,' she said. 'He did some nice studies of my face. He really *looks* when he draws.'

'Well, he has to, doesn't he.'

'No, what I mean is that he doesn't show off with style, he's modest and respectful and plays it straight.'

'Funny – I've never thought of Brian as modest.'

'When you've known somebody for a long time you get used to seeing them always the same way and you might not notice that they've changed. Brian thinks the world of you.'

'I know.'

'How is it with you and Ockerman? Still too soon to say?'

'I don't know – maybe too late.'

'If they both disappeared by magic and you could make only one of them reappear by pushing a button, which one would it be?'

'The one that's no work,' I said.

'Well, there you have it,' said Grace. 'Let me buy you a drink. What's your pleasure?'

'Thank you. I wouldn't mind a dry martini – the American kind that's mostly gin with just a little vermouth and an olive.'

'That sounds radical,' said Grace.

'This is a time for radical decisions,' I said.

'Radical martini coming up,' said Grace. 'And I'll have a vodka to keep you company because it's that kind of day. You stay put and I'll fetch the drinks.'

When she came back with the martini and the vodka and a couple of packets of crisps she said, 'What'll we drink to?'

'Absent friends?'

'Good one,' said Grace. 'Absent friends!'

The absent friend I was thinking of was Brian. After work I didn't go to my place and I didn't go to Phil's. I went to Cheyne Walk and stood at the door. If he's in and alone when I ring the bell, I thought, that's it. I rang the bell and he came down and opened the door. 'Hello,' I said. 'Can I come in?'

Later, as we lay comfortably together watching the sky darken to evening I said, 'Did you think you'd ever see me again?'

'Yes,' he said. 'I had no idea when or how but I couldn't believe you'd be out of my life for ever.'

'You feel like home.'

'That's how you feel to me. Have you . . .?'

'Ended it with Phil? I have to tell him but I don't think he'll be surprised.'

When I rang Phil up he said, 'Is this a Dear John call?'

'Were you expecting one?'

'Yes. I felt it coming on when we were eating the pizza.'

'I don't know what to say.'

'You don't have to say anything. It was just one of those things, just one of those crazy things – a trip to the moon on Barbara Strozzi. Now you're Bertha Strunk again.'

'I feel so sad, Phil.'

'I think you probably feel more relieved than sad. Let's not try too hard for an exit line – we can nod and smile if we pass each other in the street but for now let's just say goodbye.'

'Goodbye,' I said, and he rang off. Brian was down in the studio; I was alone, so I cried for a while, remembering what Phil and I had been to each other – what I *thought* we'd been anyhow – remembering what we'd said and done. And felt? Were my feelings real? Was *I* real, or just some kind of machine that did whatever it had to do to gain its objective. Shitty! And scary. And very, very sad. I was a selfish bitch who'd dropped Phil because life was easier with Brian but all I had now was sadness and I didn't know if I'd ever feel good again.

I I

PHIL OCKERMAN

I was sitting in Caffè Nero with an espresso for an excuse to sit there and I was trying on different ways to feel. Suicidal? Relieved? Numb? While I was doing that a thought came out of the closet in my head where it had been hiding: I'd said to myself that I wasn't going to write about Bertha/Barbara and me but now I thought why the hell not? Surely I was owed *that* much. While thinking about it with my eyes closed I might have dozed off a little when I heard a chair scrape back as someone sat down opposite me. I opened my eyes and there was Mimi with a cappuccino.

'What are you doing here?' I said.

'I come here every now and then wondering if you might turn up.'

'Why?'

'Sometimes I do things for no reason.' She was wearing a very conspicuous brooch copied from William

Holman Hunt's painting of the scapegoat that is driven out to the demon of the wilderness.

'Azazel,' I said.

'That's me,' said Mimi, 'waiting in the wilderness. Are you in the wilderness?'

'I don't want to be rude but what's it to you?'

'Oh come on, Phil, loosen up. I'm interested in your career.'

'Oh really! Aren't you the ex-wife who told me I was running out of ideas?'

'I said *maybe* you were. That's not to say I wasn't interested.'

'So what's your particular interest right now?'

'Don't be so defensive. Can't we just sit here and chat like old acquaintances?'

'Not yet,' I said. 'I'm off.' And I left, angry with myself because sitting there with her had been like comfortable old times. Mimi was the one who'd wanted the divorce. She'd said that living with me was too depressing. So why had she married me? We'd met at the preview of *The Genius of Rome* exhibition at the Royal Academy. We had both paused at Leonard Bramer's *The Fall of Simon Magus*. The card explained that Peter the Apostle commanded the devils who were raising Simon Magus to let go and he fell to earth.

'That hardly seems fair,' I said. 'Where would anybody in the arts be, Leonard Bramer included, without the help of devils?'

'Are you in the arts?' she said, obligingly responding to my pawn-to-king-four opening. So I told her I was a writer and was delighted to hear that she'd read my last novel. One thing led to another; over the following months we had many conversations about books and music, paintings and films. We were both keen on George Eliot and had given up on Woody Allen so we had something to build on. Plus my status as a rising novelist. It was when I fell to earth on three consecutive flights that she began to find me depressing and now we were each other's exes. I was the same failure she'd given up on so I was justifiably sceptical of her present overtures. I didn't trust her and I didn't trust myself.

What kind of relationship had we had, actually, even before I became boring? Back when I was the successful rising novelist she managed to make me feel that she was the judge of what I was and what I wasn't. I showed her my pages, looked for her approval and welcomed her comments. It was very comfortable and it made me feel less of a man and ashamed. I realised now that she needed to be the one who judged – if she were shut out from that position she didn't know what to do with herself. Did I want to go back to how things used to be? Not likely.

I couldn't stop thinking about the woman who was still Barbara to me. It seemed impossible to me that she could have said and done all those things only to use me to get rid of Troy Wallis. When I was leaving for Diamond Heart and said I'd be faithful to her because I didn't want to break the connection she'd wanted to let my words linger in her ear! She'd wanted us to walk around in each other's heads while I was gone! Well, that was then and this was now. Work was the sovereign remedy so I started making notes for my next big thing. Would it be a put-together thing trying to pass itself off as a novel? Too soon to say but it felt good to be back at work. The doorbell rang. That would be Mimi looking for a piece of the action. I buzzed her in.

'You're working again!' she said.

'So it seems,' I said.

'Are you going to let me see pages?'

'No.'

'Why not?'

'Because that's how it is now: you're not my wife, you're not my editor and you're not my friend. You dumped me when you rated me a failure and now you find that you need to get back into your old position as critic and mentor. That's not going to happen, so it's time for you to move on and find a new interest.' As I said that it hit me that it had probably been she who bailed me out.

Mimi drew herself up like a column of mercury rising in a thermometer. 'OK, champ,' she said. 'You're on your own,' and left.

I have to admit that I experienced a sudden droppedness, and at the same time an untethered-balloon sensation that left me drifting helplessly over land and sea until I was out of sight. 'Steady the buffs!' I said to myself. Kipling?

I found myself at the word machine without knowing how I'd got there. The cursor was flickering at me like the tongue of an adder. 'All right already,' I said, and typed:

MY TANGO WITH BARBARA STROZZI

1
PHIL OCKERMAN

When she told me that her name was Bertha Strunk I said, 'Is Bertha's trunk anything like Pandora's box?'
  'That isn't something you can find out in five minutes,' she said. This was at the Saturday evening tango class for beginners in the crypt of St James's Church, Clerkenwell . . .

That looked like a pretty good beginning to me; got you right into the thing and made you want to know what was coming next. Next came Mimi with her greeting about my terrible reviews: some opposition for the protagonist. The dialogue flowed nicely and then we were back in the tango lesson and I felt the solid warmth of Bertha Strunk under my hand as we carefully moved our beginners' feet to the knowing rhythm of 'La Cumparsita'. Typing out the words I lived it again and lifted my right hand to her absent back. How could she be gone! It was like a stone in my stomach. The reality and non-reality of it were too much for me. '"*And wylt thow leave me thus?*"' I said. '"*Say nay, say nay . . .*"' And then of course I had to get Sir Thomas Wyatt off the shelf:

> And wylt thow leve me thus?
>   Say nay, say nay, ffor shame,
>   To save thee from the Blame
>   Of all my greffe and grame,
> And wylt thow leve me thus?
>   Say nay, say nay!

Then of course up jumped Rabbi Moshe Leib wagging a finger and saying, 'Nu? And did you bear the burden of her sorrow?'

I thought I had, but who can know the nature and extent of another person's sorrow? I had been working towards an objective and I'd seen everything in that frame of reference. When Troy Wallis was dead I was left with the realisation that I really didn't know love at all. The walls were closing in on me so I went out.

I walked up the North End Road and stood opposite the door of the building where she no longer lived. I thought of our first kiss and how unsimple that had been. 'Nothing is simple,' I told myself, 'and you might as well accept that as a working premise.'

'OK,' I said, 'I accept it. Now what?' As if I could track the answer physically I went into the Underground and travelled to Farringdon. When I got out of the train the Yahoo ad on the wall opposite the platform was still there saying FOUND. Outside the station the headline at the news kiosk said OCKERMAN BE-REFT. The street lamps were still overwhelmed by the darkness but over the road the clustered lights and colours of FOOD & WINE, Fruit & Veg beckoned along with the Bagel Factory: the American Original. At the Chariots minicab stand the same four men stood waiting. How long since my last visit? Months? Years? Time seemed a matter of opinion and I had none. At Cowcross Street cows still refused to appear.

What was Bertha/Barbara doing while I was doing this? Posing naked for Brian? Lying naked with him? I clenched my fists as I reached the corner of Turnmill Street with the Castle Pub burnished with vertical gleamings in the dark. The people inside, were all of them happy? No, I couldn't be the only bereft one in the world. Next as I entered Turnmill *Pret A Manger* featured sushi and espresso as in the near or distant past, whichever. Then Ember with a free-standing menu that said *'Dust 'n' Ashes' Fresh daily*.

As before, I left the zone of conviviality and crossed to the left side of the street. Below me on the left the long shape of the main line showed its dim blind lights as I was swallowed up in the visible darkness. My mind brings up the same words or songs when I revisit a place, so now it gave me, as before:

The moon's my constant Mistrisse
And the lowlie owle my morrowe,
The flaming Drake and the Nightcrowe make
Mee musicke to my sorrowe.

As before, there was no moon.

The voices and laughter and music not of this time had stopped only a moment ago and now the silence rose up tumultuous. From Benjamin Street on the opposite side came volleys of reproach from left-handed slingers. Turk's Head Yard knotted me in intricacies of regret. Slightly downhill on Turnhill became, as before, slightly uphill as I neared Clerkenwell Road. Turned right into Clerkenwell Road, then crossed into Clerkenwell Close where the Crown Tavern beckoned but carried on and around a dark corner and there was St James's Church high above the rest of London, its spire aimed at the night sky where my Moon was opposed by Pluto, there was possible action pending from dangerous females, things looked generally dodgy and it behoved me to watch my ass.

'Now what?' I said to myself.

'How about work?' was my answer. So I went home and took up my narrative following the tango lesson and carrying on through my telling Bertha about *The Rainmaker* and our first kiss. The future had seemed bright then. And now the Louisville Slugger stood in its corner unused and Bertha/Barbara was gone. No matter how many times I said that to myself I couldn't accept it as reality.

12

BERTHA STRUNK

Life with Brian was all that I expected it to be. We were comfortable in every way and the improvement in his work was impressive. But I was feeling two different kinds of guilt. There was the obvious one from how I'd ill-used Phil and there was the ingrained one of my Protestant Work Ethic; I was shirking a heavy job and I was ashamed of my laziness. Living with a writer who wrote boring would be hard work but where is it written that life was meant to be easy? Maybe I could get used to it, like bad breath or premature ejaculation. Or maybe he might get into less boring – you never can tell.

Brian could see that I wasn't easy in my mind. 'Maybe,' he said, 'it would help if we took a little break.'

'I don't know,' I said.

'We could go to Paris for a few days or a week. How about it?'

'I guess I could get a week off.'

'Good. As soon as you give me the word I'll book us on Eurostar and into a hotel.'

So I talked to Karl and Georg and the following Monday we were on the train and there was that little travel-thrill to take my mind off my troubles. London zipped past, then Kent, then came the darkness of the tunnel, then France.

When we pulled into the Gare du Nord I felt as if we were really away from what we'd left behind. The sounds and echoes were full of farawayness; the roman numerals on the old clock told a different time. We queued for a taxi with smiling patience, no hurry. 'De Fleurie Hôtel,' Brian said to the driver. To me he said, 'I think you'll like it. It's in St Germain des Près, the Latin Quarter. For your first time in Paris, the Left Bank is a good place to start.'

'Have you stayed at this hotel before?' I said.

'No,' he said, 'but I Googled very carefully and looked at photos.' It was a sunny day and Paris was delightful as it went past the taxi windows. The three-star hotel was as charming as advertised and from our window we could look across the river to the Eiffel Tower. We had champagne with our dinner and the whole thing felt a little like trying too hard but I was willing to try.

Brian made a big effort – we went to a lot of places and did a lot of things but most of it was lost on me in my current frame of mind. In any case I'm not good tourist material; I tend to fasten on one thing and let everything else pass me by. It was the gargoyles of Notre Dame that got to me. We earned a close view of them by a long weary climb up hundreds of steps, even as far as the great bells. Then out into the air with all Paris spread below and the gargoyles looking out on their domain. For me they are the true soul of Notre Dame, these stone creatures that seem to hold in themselves all the sorrow and cruelty of life and the world. Also the sorrow and cruelty of God, maybe, who put into human minds the idea of these animals and demons, especially the one who's eating a human victim like a banana while others brood and think their stone thoughts high above their city.

We climbed up to Sacré Coeur, we rode down the Seine in a *bateau mouche*, we walked in the Tuileries and the Luxembourg Gardens. We dined at charming little restaurants and drank a lot of wine, some of it in the Place de Vosges with bags of pistachio nuts. We visited the Jeu de Paume, the Musée Rodin (I liked Camille Claudel's work better than his), the Musée Carnavalet and the Musée d'Orsay. We went to the Louvre but only to the bookshop – the rest of it was too crowded. In the Musée d'Orsay there's a large Daumier sketch of Don Quixote and Sancho Panza encountering a dead ass.

'Daumier!' said Brian, 'there's nobody like him. His Quixote paintings are his best work. There's an oil sketch in a book I have at home, Quixote and Sancho on Rosinante and Dapple – it's nothing but light and shadow. The gridwork Daumier used for transferring his sketches is clearly visible, and the Don and Rosinante are leaning through it as if moving into the fourth dimension. It's absolutely a metaphysical painting. We'll visit his tomb when we go to Père Lachaise. And while we're there you can also put flowers in Victor Noir's hat and rub his boots and crotch for luck.'

'Who's Victor Noir?'

'He was a young journalist shot in 1870 by Pierre Bonaparte. The story (unauthenticated) is that he was caught with Bonaparte's wife.'

'Why would I rub his boots and his crotch for luck?'

'Thousands do – you'll see when we're at his tomb.'

The next day after lunch at a brasserie we took the Metro to Père Lachaise and walked down the Boulevard Ménilmontant to the entrance where Brian bought a map of the cemetery and I bought a yellow rose.

'Have you got someone in mind for that?' he said.

'I don't know yet.'

The morning had been sunny but the sky had become grey and overcast; an air of gentle melancholy pervaded the place and I found it very comfortable.

' "He that dies this year is quit for the next," ' quoted Brian. 'Everyone here is a fully paid-up mortal. They died peacefully or violently, publicly or privately, famously or obscurely, and here they lie, each with a name and number on the map. But not all who died here have names and numbers: for some there's only a wall, the Mur des Fédérés: hundreds of members of the Paris Commune were stood up against it in 1871 and shot in batches. I read in *Frommer's* that a handful survived and lived in the vaults like wild animals for years. They'd come out at night to forage for food in Paris. *Frommer's* doesn't say what happened to their bodies when they died.'

'They must be ghosts now,' I said, 'and probably they're known by name to the other ghosts: Héloïse and Abelard,' I read, 'Chopin, Jane Avril but no Toulouse-Lautrec. Here's Daumier next to Corot at *vingt-qua-trième.*'

'Jim Morrison is here too,' said Brian. 'He pulls the most visitors.'

'He's probably the life of the party after midnight.'

'More like *all* night; I'm sure they rock around the clock. Look at the names on the map – it's a pretty wild crowd here.'

We made our way up Avenue Saint-Morys, did a right, and there was the flat grey slab that said:

DAUMIER
Honoré Victorin
N. Marseilles Fevrier 26 1808
M. Valmondois Fevrier 10 1879

Madame DAUMIER
Née Marie Alexandrine
DASSY
N. Paris Fevrier 2 1822
M. Paris Janvier 11 1895

'*Bonjour, Monsieur, Madame,*' said Brian. '*Tout va bien?*' He brushed off the slab with his hand and took a notebook from his pocket. He wrote in it, tore off the page, put it on the tomb and weighted it with a pebble. 'Thank you note,' he said. '*À bientôt,*' he said to the Daumiers as we left. 'Victor Noir next.'

We turned right on to Avenue Transversale No. 1, took a left into Avenue Greffulhe, and there was Victor flat on his back with a bullet hole in his chest and a bulge in his trousers. 'Died with a hard-on,' said Brian. 'Tough one, Vic.' To me he said, 'Perhaps you'd like a few minutes alone with him?'

'Thanks,' I said. 'I would.' Brian withdrew and I stood looking down at the life-size bronze figure. It was a little startling at first, as if he had been shot only a moment ago. His coat and jacket were opened, his shirt was unbuttoned, exposing the bullet-hole, his trousers had been loosened, and his crotch and boots were well burnished by the hands of female visitors. His top hat lay by his right side with roses and cards in it. There was a bouquet by his left hand. I kissed my yellow rose and put it in his hat. I rubbed his erection and his boot, said, 'Anything you can do, Victor,' blew him a kiss and joined Brian.

'Père Lachaise is a good pick-up place,' he said. 'You can find whatever kind of woman you're looking for here.'

'Live ones?'

'Very.'

'Have you picked up any?'

'Not lately. Is there anyone else here you'd like to drop in on?'

I thought of Jane Avril with her long face and her high-kicking leg in the Lautrec poster but I decided to keep that image in my mind rather than her tomb so we headed back to the Boulevard Ménilmontant. The cemetery was full of trees and shadows. I recognised the yew and the rowan, not the others. The sun came out and the monuments went pale.

We had dinner at Les Deux Magots and took an evening stroll through the Latin Quarter before going back to the hotel. This was our last evening in Paris. We'd made love on the first couple of nights but not since. 'One has the feeling that the thrill is gone,' said Brian.

'Protestant Work Ethic,' I said. 'I don't feel right when life is easy.'

We checked out the next morning. We never did go up the Eiffel Tower.

13

PHIL OCKERMAN

The Coroner's Inquest came up and Barbara – I can't keep calling her Bertha/Barbara – was there. What can I say? My heart skipped a beat when I saw her. She gave me a really sweet look and said, 'Hi, Phil. How's it going?'

'Pages are happening,' I said. 'How's it with you?'

'You know – same old eyeballs. You've got a new novel going! I'm really glad to hear that.'

'Still with Brian?'

'No, actually.'

At this point there were three knocks and the Coroner's Officer said, 'Rise, please, to Her Majesty's Coroner.' We rose as the Coroner came in. 'Oyez, oyez, oyez,' said the Coroner's Officer as the Coroner passed to the bench, 'all manner of persons who have anything to do at this court before the Queen's Coroner touching upon the death of Troy Hector Wallis draw near and give your attendance. Pray be seated.'

The Coroner's Court in Fulham is shaped like a large telephone box, and my thoughts rose up vertically both inside and outside of it. The clear grey light that came in through the windows was cool and sceptical. Possibly it had heard too many lies to take anything for granted. Ten Bibles in the jury box, two more by the witness box. There was a poor box by the door. Behind the Coroner the royal arms said DIEU ET MON DROIT.

As all the persons having anything to do etc. drew near and gave their attendance we were sworn in and testified that everything had happened the way it had happened. Then the Coroner returned a verdict of accidental death, Bob was our uncle, and there we were out on the street blinking in the sunlight.

Barbara and I were looking at each other as if our mouths had forgotten how to form words. Eventually we both spoke at the same time: 'Maybe . . .' was our joint utterance.

'You first,' said Barbara.

'Maybe,' I said, 'we could have dinner one evening?'

'That's what I was going to say.'

'Tonight?'

'I can't. I'm going from here to Paddington to get a train for Exeter. My parents and I have never been very close but my father is in hospital for heart surgery and I told my mother I'd be there. If all goes well I'll probably be back in a week. Can we not talk on the phone while I'm away and can I walk around in your head?'

'Please walk on in and set right down and make yourself at home,' I said.

We took the Underground together and at the station we kissed goodbye but it was definitely a hello kiss. When I got home I sat down at the word machine and words began appearing on the screen as if my story were heading for someplace good. I poured myself a large Laphroaig, said, 'Here's luck!' and let my fingers dance over the keys for a good three hours. I was enjoying myself; I particularly liked the part where we watched *The Rainmaker* video and I was still smiling about it when I got into bed.

True to her word, Barbara came and walked around in my head. She seemed totally comfortable in herself and with me. 'It's nice to be here,' she said. 'I guess it's pretty much my favourite place. Being with Brian just wasn't right for me. I've given us a lot of thought, and I think what you and I have between us is something we'll never find again with anyone else. Do you agree?'

'Emphatically.'

'I know it won't be easy. It used to bother me a lot that you write boring but I think I can handle that now. I mean, it's no worse than watching football on TV all the time or losing the housekeeping playing poker.'

'That's very generous of you,' I said, 'but it could be that I won't always write boring.'

'Whatever,' said Barbara. 'I just want you to know I'm in this for the long haul.'

'I know,' I said. 'When I went to St James's Clerkenwell for that tango lesson I could feel that Barbara Strozzi was with me, and when I saw your face, sad and beautiful like her music, I knew that you'd be with me from then on. She's with both of us now, still sad, still wanting someone to know her needs and bear the burden of her sorrow.'

'Still wanting so long after her death?'

'I don't think the wanting ever stops.'

'Well, we can take her along with us, can't we?'

'All the way, Barb.'

'That's settled then. How are things with you in general?'

'Work's been going well,' I said. 'I'll have some pages to show you when you get back.'

There was a little pause at her end, then she said, 'I look forward to reading them. I'll say goodnight now.' She kissed me and left and I drifted off to sleep smiling.

Barbara showed up in my head every night while she was in Exeter. No heavy schmoozing – we just talked about all kinds of things from hair styles to dishwashers. She rang me up a week after she'd left to tell me that her father had come safely through the operation and she'd be coming home in two days. 'I'll call again to let you know what train I'll be on,' she said.

She arrived on a Tuesday evening. I met her off the train and we went to a little French restaurant in the North End Road. 'My last French restaurant was Les Deux Magots,' she said.

'How *was* Paris?'

'It wasn't where I wanted to be.'

She stayed at my place that night and the next day we moved her in after work. I'd given up my classes, so my time was my own. I had enough in the bank to get me through six months and now with her salary added to it we could last maybe a year without any new income. I thought I had a pretty good chance of finishing *My Tango with Barbara Strozzi* and getting an advance by then. The pages were marching right along; I was doing my chapters in alternate first-person narration so of course I had to imagine Barbara's part of it. When I'd got to p 92, which felt like somewhere past halfway, I was ready to show her what I'd done so far.

After dinner one evening I put the ms in her hands; we got to the HMS *Victory* part and as she reached the end of p 92 she said, 'I have good feelings about this. Do you know how it's going to end?'

'Not yet,' I said.

'Hey,' said Barbara, 'it didn't bore me at all! You think this might be a turning point?'

'You never know.'

She went to the fridge and came back with a bottle of Moët & Chandon. I opened it and poured and we raised our glasses.

'You know, Phil,' said Barbara, 'I don't believe there's anyone who could know my needs and bear the burden of my sorrow the way you do.'

'I'll drink to that,' I said, 'and I feel the same about you.'

'Here's to Barbara Strozzi,' said Barbara, and we clinked.

'And Neptune and Pluto and all those other planets who have been active on our behalf,' I said.

'And us,' said Barbara.

'And us,' said I.

ACKNOWLEDGMENTS

Catriona Mundle was the astrologer not only for the people in this story but also for me. Her horoscopes consistently offered useful insights as I worked.

Rob Warren of the Greenwich Observatory gave me astronomical guidance.

Amanda Peiro, whom I had consulted about tango in a previous novel, referred me to her father, Teddy Peiro, who sent me tango material and put me on to Paul Lange and Michiko Ukazaki and their tango classes at St James's Church, Clerkenwell. Paul and Michiko also helped me with a private session at their house; Christine Denniston's CD-ROM, *Dancing Tango*, was my source for most of the tango history in the text; the three *Argentine Tango* CD-ROMs with Christy Cote and George Garcia which Phil used were from The Tango Catalogue (US); Helena of totaltango very carefully selected tango recordings for me which had the authentic sound I wanted to hear.

Lara Hoffenberg of the University of Cape Town generously provided extensive information about South Africa and patiently answered all my questions. Lebethe Malefo graciously translated 'Used To Be' into Setswana and sent me a recording of him speaking the song.

Thank you! to Alice.

Miela Ford, ocularist, was my source for details of that profession.

My rabbis were drawn from Martin Buber's *Tales of the Hasidim*.

This is not the place for a bibliography but I must say how inspiriting I found Adam Nicolson's *Men of Honour: Trafalgar and the Making of an English Hero*. And the reality of my visit to HMS *Victory* in Portsmouth was augmented and recalled vividly to life by the beautiful HMS *Victory: Her Construction, Career and Restoration* by Alan McGowan. *Nelson's Navy: The Ships, Men and Organisation 1793–1815* by Brian Lavery is a longtime resident of my maritime library and an invaluable aid in visualising the ships and the action of the period.

Dominic Power read my pages as I wrote them and reliably made useful comments.

My wife Gundula Hoban, as always, kept me up to date with fashion details and London in general.

R.H.
London 2007

A NOTE ON THE AUTHOR

Russell Hoban is the author of many extraordinary novels including *Turtle Diary*, *Riddley Walker*, *Amaryllis Night and Day*, *The Bat Tattoo*, *Her Name Was Lola*, *Come Dance With Me* and, most recently, *Linger Awhile*. He has also written some classic books for children including *The Mouse and his Child* and the *Frances* books. He lives in London.

A NOTE ON THE TYPE

The text of this book is set in Bembo. This type was first
used in 1495 by the Venetian printer Aldus Manutius for Cardinal
Bembo's *De Aetna*, and was cut for Manutius by Francesco
Griffo. It was one of the types used by Claude Garamond
(1480–1561) as a model for his Romain de L'Université,
and so it was the forerunner of what became standard European
type for the following two centuries. Its modern form
follows the original types and was designed for
Monotype in 1929.